A SÉANCE FOR
WICKED KING DEATH

A SÉANCE FOR WICKED KING DEATH

by Coy Hall

SHOTGUN HONEY
2023

Published by **Shotgun Honey Books**

215 Loma Road
Charleston, WV 25314
www.ShotgunHoney.com

Cover Design by Ron Earl Phillips.

First Printing 2023.

ISBN-10: 1-956957-22-7
ISBN-13: 978-1-956957-22-8

9 8 7 6 5 4 3 2 1   23 22 21 20 19 18

For Olivia & Locksley

A SÉANCE FOR WICKED KING DEATH

The Marley Caldwell Palace of Motion Pictures was a lot of name for a second-run theater on the edge of East 14th and Sycamore Street. The building had size to justify the name, but it was an old, unkempt, and seedy palace. The implied glamour didn't shine through. Most of the bulbs on the marquee were dead, with some of the lights busted to the rim. The front doors sagged on rusted hinges and came together like crowded teeth. The theater had meant something in the twenties, but decay began when the city shifted northward after the war. When I started work there as a factotum (ushering, selling tickets, and cleaning), the theater was a run-down hangout for James Dean types and Korean War vets addicted to heroin.

Although I wasn't much on scrubbing toilets, ushering wasn't a bad gig. The pay was nothing, but I stole time to watch the movies. I'm a fan enough of pictures to buy star magazines, so watching was the main perk of the job. I'd grown up on matinee pictures and serials in the thirties. My mother used a theater as a nanny. That's why I worked at the Marley Caldwell and not the hot peanut and cigarette stand next door, or at any of the bars up and down East 14th.

Being October, and only a month since Bela Lugosi's death

made the papers, the Caldwell got by with showing a rerun double bill of the old *Dracula* and *Frankenstein* pictures.

On that particular night, I'd been ushering, drifting in and out of the theater, admiring the screen and the tones of "Swan Lake" more than stabbing my flashlight at the rowdy patrons (and they were young tonight), when Anna Vogel came running into the lobby. She was breathless, pale, and fresh off the cold street. Seeing her there, I had a moment. A blitz of memories surfaced. This was someone I considered to be from another life, someone I thought I'd never see again, and seeing her shocked my system. I hadn't seen Anna in nine years, not since we'd performed séances together on the carnival circuit. That would've been 1947, just after the war.

Anna had a wild look in her eyes. She breathed like she'd been running for blocks. She sprinted toward me as if she knew I'd be in that spot at that moment. I'm not paranoid, but it wasn't serendipitous. Someone told her where and when I worked. She ran at me and grabbed hold like a scared child. I emptied my hands, putting aside the flashlight and sticking the burning Chesterfield in my mouth. I wrapped my arms around her. She shook all the way through. Her arms were like ice, bumps raised. Her wavy blonde hair brushed my chin. It was brittle with hairspray, and a hint of soured strawberry infused the aroma.

No one would call me a therapist, but, in my old line of business, I'd seen my share of hysterical people. When you do séances and tell fortunes, you see people in the doldrums, often distraught. I didn't shower Anna with questions. I gave her the moment and hugged her for as long as she needed it. When her grip softened, I flicked my cigarette, spilling ash on the old red carpet, and offered her what remained.

She accepted the stick and took a long drag. Her hands

were lily white with yellow tar stains around the nails. The cigarette put blood in her face. Crimson emerged beneath her cheekbones. She looked up with catlike eyes, and for a moment the eyes looked less dead than the ocean floor. Anna hadn't changed much since I'd seen her last, but the lines around her eyes and mouth had deepened. She must've been close to forty, yet she looked older.

"It's been a while, Anna," I said. I tried to be wry, to smile and make her smile, but she was overwrought.

She looked at and through me, and then she stared at the front doors of the lobby, where posters of silent films lined the walls. Everybody was in the auditorium. The concessions stood empty. A few notes of music trickled through the curtains.

Anna finished the cigarette and threw the remains aside. I pulled a pack from my coat and offered another. She took the stick, and I lit it. We stood like that for a couple minutes. I tried to be patient, but shock gave way to curiosity. Mr. Pedersoli, the Caldwell's owner, watched us through the glass of his ticket booth.

I grabbed Anna's free hand, which was a block of ice. Her fingers trembled.

"Royce," she said grimly, "I need your help." Although she conveyed it was difficult to ask such a thing, I knew Anna too well. She had no trouble asking anybody for anything at anytime. Anna always needed help, and she was always willing to ask.

I squeezed to warm her hand.

She pulled loose. She exhaled a cloud of smoke and crossed her arms. It was night and cold, yet she didn't wear a coat. I had the sense she didn't own one, because her clothes were moth-eaten.

"For starters, I need you to hide me," she said. Her tone was colorless, unnaturally level, as if she were trying not to cry.

One likes to think he'd say heroic things in such a situation, but I managed much less. I asked, rather foolishly, "Right now?"

Anxiously, Anna looked toward the entrance. The boss, red-faced and bearded Mr. Pedersoli, was selling tickets tonight. For the moment, he'd stopped watching us. He buried his nose in a Gold Medal paperback.

Anna handed over the unfinished cigarette and nodded. "Right now."

An odd thought occurred to me. Anna Vogel, although she had more age on her, was a remarkable likeness of Mina in *Dracula*, which played on the screen at that very moment. The resemblance was uncanny, and I'd never noticed it before.

"He can't be far," Anna said. "When he comes in here looking for me, I want you to lie. I need it, Royce. It's a big favor, but I need it, old boy."

Old boy. I'd forgotten that. She used those old phrases to add a touch of elegance to her persona. She was a child of the gutter, but in her mind she came from old money. She could only hide poverty from her fellow paupers, though. Nobody else fell for it, no matter how many *old boys* she dropped.

"Okay, I haven't seen you," I said. I didn't know what else to do or say.

She watched me. "I mean it. Tell him what you have to tell him, but you haven't seen me, not in years."

"That's about half right anyway," I said. "Who is he?"

She didn't divulge that information. "You won't miss him. He's wearing a suit and jacket. How many come in here wearing a tie?"

"Very few," I admitted.

"Even if he gives you the third degree, Royce, you gotta lie. You haven't seen me."

"He isn't a cop, is he? I don't want anything to do with cops."

"He ain't no cop."

"Are you going to tell me who he is?"

"Later," Anna said impatiently. "I'll tell you everything later."

I nodded, threw yet another stub on the ground, and then I pulled Anna toward the darkness of the theater and sounds of *Dracula*. I found a place where she could sit alone, away from the delinquents. There were a lot of bad seeds in the crowd tonight, ribbing one another, throwing popcorn around, putting knives in the seats, talking to the screen.

To my relief, nobody except a few kids came through the front door for the remainder of the night. The prowler with a tie never showed. Waiting frayed my nerves, though. On edge, I chain-smoked a pack of Chesterfields, missing out on the movies, surveilling the entrance like a watchman.

CHAPTER TWO

When Mr. Pedersoli caught me preparing to leave with Anna for the night, he strolled over.

"Hey there," he said to the girl, winking.

A knowing grin crossed his face. He whispered about being hornier than a fifty-piece brass band, loud enough so Anna would hear, and I treated him like you treat people who pay you: I laughed, too. He smelled of department store cologne, talcum powder, and sweat. No matter the weather, Mr. Pedersoli sweated through his clothes. Large, damp rings remained in the armpits of his shirts. I didn't dislike the man, he had his charms.

"You have to watch those nympho novels," I said. "They'll do that to you."

The cover of the book he'd consumed tonight showed a redhead in negligee, pining, while three bulging studs waited in line at her door. Her bed was disheveled like a football game occurred on it. It wasn't the first time Mr. Pedersoli had read that sensitive portrayal of womanhood. It was well thumbed.

"You ain't kiddin'," he said, guffawing. "Funnels your blood, if you know how I mean." With his hands, he showed me how he meant it. He was fat enough that laughing made him sweat more. He pawed at his brow. If placed on the sidewalk, the man would've steamed like a dog dropped him.

Since he enjoyed the date angle, I made the most of it. "Mr. Pedersoli, how about an advance on my pay this week?"

I'd never asked for an advance before, and yet he changed his mood, completely and utterly, and he frowned.

"What do you need?"

I nodded toward Anna, who waited near the exit with her arms folded. "I can't exactly drag her to Angelo's, can I?"

Mr. Pedersoli looked at Anna and considered. She didn't have much more class than the clientele at Angelo's, but I could envision him churning out a chestnut like *love is blind*. He pulled out a fiver, folded three times over, and offered it.

I took the money. "Thanks, Mr. Pedersoli. I owe you."

He shrugged. "Lock the door on your way out, Royce," he said. He leaned forward and put his hand on my arm. "Enjoy it. I never see you with girls. And it looks like the spook shows got in this one's head. She'll be cake tonight, pally. She'll beg for it." With that, he turned and walked toward the projection room where Mrs. Pedersoli toiled. He was always paranoid about his wife putting away the celluloid, or so he claimed. Whatever else occurred in that room, I preferred not to know. He had that hungry look, though.

Sadly, it was the last time I saw the man.

●　●　●

The streetlight nearest the Marley Caldwell had been out for a couple months, and the city refused to fix this and other dead lights, so that left our block with large swaths of darkness. A couple lights still functioned, so it was a matter of rushing through shadows, reaching a halo, taking a breath, and then rushing again to the next. I lived near enough to the theater to walk to and from work, so I didn't own a car. Everything I needed was within a square mile, and I hadn't been adventurous for a couple years. My lack of an automobile disappointed Anna. She hoped I owned Mr. Pedersoli's big black Buick at the curb. Anna was in no mood to stroll in the dark.

With the tenement housing and junkies, East 14th was dangerous even in daylight. I was more nervous than usual with a woman at my side. Anna clutched a purse, too.

At first, we didn't say much. We just walked, our footsteps loud in the crisp air. A few cars with blinding headlights passed, but, mostly, the night was muted. It was cold enough to leave rime on windows, and a snaking breeze moved leaves and garbage around. Since my uniform consisted of a garish maroon jacket, I gave my coat to Anna. Wrapped inside, she shuddered like a kitten.

A few bars, whose neon lights shone against the sidewalk, stood a block from the theater.

"That's where we're stopping first," I said.

She didn't react.

"I can get both of us drunk with a five."

Anna nodded, agreeable but dazed. She'd slept through the entirety of *Frankenstein,* the second picture of the night. A piece of popcorn, thrown by one of the delinquents, stuck to her hair. I flicked it away. She gave me a look.

As we walked, I asked if she wanted me to hold her hand to keep it warm, and she shoved her fist into the coat pocket. Anna was a tough knot when she applied her mind to it, so I let it go.

After crossing Sycamore, we passed a park bordered by a chain link fence full of dead laurel. The playground was once part of a junior high, but the school had moved. Nothing had replaced the abandoned building, so the yard functioned as a park where children bought and sold dope. There was also a seesaw. A few squatters lived in the school behind boarded windows. I always worried a junkie would chase me down and knife me for witnessing a deal taking place. For that reason, I carried a blackjack to and from work. I'd also made a habit of looking the other way when I walked by the yard.

"Don't look over there," I said.

Of course, goaded, she looked over like she was trying to find the moon through a telescope. The cold kept everything still and quiet, though. The lot was empty tonight.

We passed Angelo's and came to a bar called The Sherwood. It was a tongue-in-cheek place with a lot of Lincoln green paint and a mural on the wall of Errol Flynn as Robin Hood and Olivia de Havilland as Maid Marian. The mural was kitsch, so I liked it. The same man who once owned the Marley Caldwell had once owned The Sherwood, and now he was dead and owned neither. Mr. Pedersoli had no interest in The Sherwood, and he was going to let it rot, so somebody bought it and turned it into a bar. It was a restaurant when the mural went up in 1938. Now, divorced from the theater, The Sherwood looked disharmonious beside a tough joint like Angelo's. Debauchery spilled over, though. Recently, some punk kids scraped Errol Flynn's eyes from the painting. A barmaid tried to improve the situation by covering the holes with boot black, and now Robin looked like a dead-soul minion of Lucifer. As we entered, I pointed this out to Anna, but she was humorless, despondent. She looked and looked away again.

The Sherwood was nearly empty, save for a few men on stools at the bar. I led Anna to a booth at the far corner. She sat down. Shadow covered her face. Light music, a recording by The Jazz Messengers, played on a jukebox behind us.

"Hang tight," I said.

From Carlo, a bartender with whom I'd made friends over the last year, I bought two gins, one with tonic and one neat, and got some change for the cigarette machine. When I returned to Anna, I had a drink and a cigarette for each of us. Her head was down on the table, and she was crying. Her back heaved as if she were short of breath. I still didn't know what was going on, so I didn't know what to make of it. I thought about pills, her old habit with barbiturates. I sat beside her. I patted her back.

Anna took the gin and tonic and downed it. I lit her cigarette. She leaned back in the seat, loosened the coat. She wiped the makeup around her eyes and tried to still her breath. She fended off a panic attack. She looked like hell.

"Why don't you tell me about it?" I asked. I sipped the gin. The first taste went through me like morning coffee. After a strange night, I needed the feeling. I tasted it again and exhaled around it, trying to enjoy it.

"Why'd you leave the business, Royce?" Anna asked.

She meant the business we shared, that of mediums. We had a good run as scammers. For those inclined to litigate: entertainers. For those with a moral compass: predators. We pretended to speak to the dead. Despite what the boogeymen researchers at the Duke Parapsychology Labs said, genuine mediums existed only in fiction. The dead didn't speak.

I hadn't done that type of work in years.

I lit my cigarette then and shrugged. I exhaled through my nose and took another drink. "I got burned one too many times," I said, which was true. "They put me away two years, you know? Up at Mansfield." I flicked ashes. It was part of my record, part of my existence now. I was an ex-con. Mr. Pedersoli knew about it. I hadn't lied to him.

"I remember," Anna said. "I cut it out of the newspaper when it happened."

I smiled, took another drag. "Did you really?"

She nodded.

"I'd like to see that."

"It was just after we'd finished a circuit. It scared me."

"More like a couple years after."

"You know what else I cut out of the paper?"

"Good Christ, don't tell me."

"I did," she said. "For a while I kept Frank O'Shaughnessy's article about you."

Smoke escaped as I laughed, but the memory hurt. I leaned back against the cushioned seat. Frank O'Shaughnessy was a writer at the *Cincinnati Enquirer*. He had a weekly column on bad businesses, con artists, and the like. It was tabloid stuff. O'Shaughnessy was snide and mean-spirited and popular, and he was just as much a predator as those whom he damned. The series was called *Caveat Emptor* (Let the Buyer Beware), and the column still ran as far as I knew. I avoided the papers myself.

In 1950, my worst year to date, he singled me out as a threat to widows on Millionaires' Row. He knew one of the women who paid me, so he did a write up on me as a charlatan. Why he singled me out, I'm still not sure. It was his public duty, he wrote, to warn old bags not to fall for my act. He ruined me. Not long after the article, I found myself on trial for fraud. That particular case had less to do with being a medium and more with being desperate, but I digress.

"You're lucky he's never written an article about you," I said.

"You'll see business go from up here to down here." I smacked the table. "He can do that. He's got fans."

Anna recoiled at the jarring noise. A man looked over from the bar. The atmosphere was jumpy. Somebody started a new record on the jukebox, more milquetoast jazz.

"Maybe," she said. Emotion retreated from her eyes.

"I never hit pay dirt anyhow," I said. "To tell the truth, I do better working for Mr. Pedersoli."

Anna laughed at me. This was the first genuine reaction she'd given. It was a nice change.

"I don't believe that a second," she said. "We made a killing with those séances. One of the hags would've put you up on Millionaires' Row if you'd asked. You just never asked."

I tasted the gin. "You want another?" I asked.

She did, without the tonic, so I got her one like mine.

When I returned, Anna said, "I had one of your old customers on the line recently. Had her three days a week. I told her fortune with cards on Tuesdays, talked to her dead husband on Wednesdays, and talked to her dead son on Thursdays. It was steady work." She slid back the coat sleeve and showed me a gold chain on her wrist. "Bought me that," she said.

A wave of jealousy went through me. How Anna escaped the gaze of O'Shaughnessy puzzled me. There was a time when I was bitter about that fact. There was an entire community of scammers in Cincinnati, and I'd been singled out as a scapegoat. Old feelings of resentment returned.

The coat fell back into place, hiding the chain. "You remember after the war how much money we made on biddies like that?" She shook her head. She stubbed out the cigarette and laughed. "Jesus," she said.

"Was it Fawn Bailey you hooked?" I asked.

"It was indeed."

One of the cash cows, I thought. *Damn.* "I remember. She and her husband had a stake in Procter & Gamble."

Anna nodded.

"Except I talked to her son alone back then," I said. "He died in the Pacific. I had this whole yarn about him helping us beat the Japanese by confusing radio signals. Her old man was alive then. He was as big a sucker as she was. Everything I said he wrote down. At one point, he was going to make a book out of it. No kidding. That would've made me. He didn't end up doing it after O'Shaughnessy busted me. They got embarrassed and dropped me."

"That's why you were so good, old boy. You improvise when everyone else rehearses. You got imagination. It's all those movies you watch. You still a fanatic?"

"You saw where I work."

She smiled.

"I once told a story that her son, his ghost anyhow, single-handedly sank a Japanese sub. He was popping out wires and plugs. I don't even know how a damn sub works."

At that, we both laughed. For Anna, it was cathartic. That, coupled with liquor, released some of her tension. For me, it was painful and depressing.

"Do you miss it?" she asked.

I nodded. I did miss those times. Then the other side of my brain came back with a defense. I talked to convince myself more than to sway Anna.

"Prison has me gun shy," I said. "I can't go back to that. It isn't worth it." I finished the cigarette. "I can't get in trouble again."

"Maybe if you changed towns," Anna said.

I let that go, but temptation remained in the air.

"Don't tell me Mrs. Bailey sent someone chasing after you

tonight," I said. I imagined her dandified chauffeur in hot pursuit of Anna on East 14th. I laughed to myself. It was too much. Her chauffeur looked like one of the twins in the *Alice in Wonderland* cartoon.

Anna sobered, and the anxious look returned to her eyes. "Worse than that," she said. "I really stepped in a hole this time, old boy."

I watched her without saying anything.

"You remember Wendell Marsh?"

I nodded.

"He and I got together again."

I had to whistle at that. Insensitive, but it just came out. *You're daft,* I thought.

Anna and Wendell Marsh had a long history. They'd been an item off and on ever since I'd known Anna. Marsh was always a presence. He was, without mincing words, a hard-edged bastard. Although I didn't have proof, I believed him to be an enforcer for the syndicate out of Columbus. Maybe he was, or perhaps he was just violent and brutish. He was a natural thug, regardless, and he always had money without a job. I'd seen Marsh beat a man only once, a hick at the carnival who pinched the ass of a dancer, but that was all I needed to see. Marsh was cruel. Hearing his name made me nervous, and I began watching the entrance and sidewalk along with Anna.

She went on. "It's more than that. I broke it off with him last night. Nothing new, we had a row. It's a weekly thing." She lowered her voice then. "This time I took $300 in cash from his dresser."

My eyebrows knitted. "You're putting me in a danger-ous spot," I said. Wendell Marsh and I weren't friends or even friendly. He'd have no qualms about dragging me over concrete just for sitting in a booth with Anna. If he thought I played a part in stealing money from him, too…. Sweat broke out on my palms. Quite suddenly, I had no desire to be in a bar or in public or in Cincinnati, Ohio.

Anna twirled her empty glass, making a tight ring, and she stared at the table. Tears returned to her eyes.

"You have the money on you?" I asked. My voice dropped into a low register now, too. It's amazing how a simple piece of information can transform your manner. As easy as that, Anna and I were conspiring.

"Yes. I was living with him. I don't have anywhere to go with it."

The idea that she'd been walking 14th with $300 made me dizzy.

"What do you want from me? I can't hide you here. Even if I could, how long? Somebody, somewhere saw you tonight and it won't be long before Marsh knows it. Then what?"

"Royce, I want you to get me out of the city."

Goddamnit, I thought. That was the hinge moment. That was when I could have washed my hands of Anna Vogel, wished her well, slid free from the booth, and *sprinted.*

Instead of doing sensible things, I gathered myself and headed back to the bar. I gave $2.75 to Carlo for a bottle of gin to go. He put a quarter on my tab.

"Nice lookin' broad," he commented. "Enjoy it, buddy."

Enjoy it.

He and Mr. Pedersoli were thinking in the wrong direction. In hindsight, so was I. While escorting Anna out into the windy cold, with leaves from the old schoolyard swirling in the street, I felt like a gallant heart. We rushed across Sycamore and went to the nearest light. In that manner, light to light, I escorted Anna to my apartment.

CHAPTER THREE

I lived in a boarding house a couple blocks up Goetz Alley. When this section of town was clean, my building was stylish. Faced with Hummelstown brownstone and perched on the corner of East Liberty, the place possessed charm once. A charcoal print of the building tried to convince everyone that class remained, at least in the bones of the place. The print hung in the foyer beside the pay phone. It was like an old woman with a portrait of herself in youth above the fireplace. You almost believed the portrait, but you had doubts about the sincerity of the artist.

With the building's style faded, there was no waiting list for residency. Rooms were available a day or week at a time, and for only slightly more cost than tenement housing offered by the state of Ohio. Half a century of neglect left the brownstone a crumbling mess with a sagging façade. From the street, the building looked unhappy and dark. It was a matter of time before Mrs. Kohut, the landlady, torched the property for a share of the insurance money.

In the stairwell, Anna and I passed a couple of hoods smoking, but they paid little attention to us. They were high on something, spaced. I had a room on the fourth floor, the top. I brought Anna to my door. I checked over my shoulder.

The floor was quiet save for the faint noise of a radio in one of the rooms. The corridor remained empty. The hoods hadn't followed.

I took Anna's hand and pulled her along. On the walk over, she admitted she hadn't slept for more than a day, and the gin made things worse, so she looked dead, skeletal around sunken eyes. In the theater she'd taken barbiturates, I decided. I brought her inside and led her to the bedroom. I got the coat off and helped her shoes off. I put her down on the mattress and then raised her head to slip a pillow underneath. She was asleep in seconds. She turned onto her side, getting a healthy dose of makeup on the pillow, and murmured. I placed her purse at her side so it would be within reach when she needed it. I ignored an urge to peek at the $300.

With Anna out of my hair, I had time to think. I left the dark, cold bedroom and walked into the living room. Gusts rattled the thin, single-paned windows.

After replacing my usher jacket with a worn sweatshirt, I sat by my reading lamp. Usually, this was a spot of sanctuary where I hid after work. I preferred here to out there. A pile of books and magazines and a Regency transistor radio lay on the side table. These were companions. A soiled plate from last night's dinner, full of cigarette stubs, lay there, too. The sight reminded me how long it had been since I'd eaten (and how long it'd been since I'd emptied an ashtray), but I didn't feel hungry. Thankfully, I found an unfinished pack of Chesterfields among the rubble. That was a blessing.

The lamp, the couch, the plate, and the table all came with the rent (as did the single bed that Anna occupied). I owned very little, in fact: an armful of clothes and some junk strewn about.

The soft, familiar lamplight spreading over the room

brought much needed calmness. I lit a cigarette, and that, too, improved my composure. After a drink of the gin I'd bought from Carlo, I was human again. Tension drained from my shoulders. Eventually, I stopped watching the front door, waiting for a knock. I put my legs up on the couch and got comfortable. That's how I fell asleep most nights. I rarely used the bed.

Aside from the problem of Anna Vogel, I thought about a lot of things. Apparently, I was too charged to sleep, because a couple hours later I was out of cigarettes and the gin was low.

In the middle of a waking dream, I looked up to find Anna standing at the door of the bedroom. I was fairly drunk. My face was warm and heavy. She emerged from the darkness like bas-relief, her hair a nest, her feet bare (this dropped an inch from her petite stature). She reminded me of a child asking for a drink of water, too scared to be alone, afraid of the dark.

"What time is it?" she asked. Her voice, too, was small.

I dug around for the watch I used at work. "Nearly four," I said. "Ten till."

To be honest, I was thankful for the intrusion. When she'd appeared my mind was back at Mansfield with a nightmare by the name of Barnett, a man who reminded me of Wendell Marsh. Barnett was one of those hicks fashioned from granite, beaten as a kid until a thick callus covered his brain, with no teeth in his head and no prayer of leaving confinement. He'd beaten me senseless once a week for a few months. Barnett was my introduction to life at the reformatory.

Good Christ.

I'd tried to fight back, but it was useless against an animal like that. With the effect it had on Barnett, my fist might as well have been bird bones. I got to the point where I didn't want to leave my cell, not for anything. Barnett reduced me to something infantile. He moved on to another target after that, as if I bored him, but he'd left shiny scars above my eye, at the corner of my mouth, and a missing tooth as reminders. He and Marsh would've been great friends.

Anna slipped back into the darkness and then returned with her purse. She sat beside me on the couch. The springs groaned and the cushions sagged. It wasn't a comfortable piece of furniture, not for two. Anna tucked her feet beneath her for warmth.

"Have you ever seen $300 all at once?" she asked.

I had, in fact. I came from money.

She reached over and took the gin from the table. She gulped down a healthy dram from the bottle. After handing back the liquor, she fished a wad of bills from the purse. I put the gin aside, knocking some magazines to the floor.

Anna slid back, putting a cushion between us. Then, with showmanship, she placed the bills president up like they were tarot cards. One at a time, she smoothed the folds. The $300 was entirely in twenties, so fifteen bills lay on the cushion when she finished: eight on top and seven on the bottom, arranged like a squat T.

"You must feel like Little Caesar," I said. "That's what they call New York confetti."

Anna flashed the grin of a gun moll. I'd seen the look before, but it was on Jean Harlow in a Jimmy Cagney movie. Anna only needed a silk dress and earrings. She already had that prewar platinum hair. Unlike Ms. Harlow, Anna's dark roots peaked through.

"How come you trust me so much?" I asked.

That had been on my mind. Being drunk dropped my inhibitions about asking. When we worked together, we were never close enough to be confidants. We shared no secrets.

Yet, here she was, completely exposed, unfettered, placing everything in the open for me to see. Certainly, I didn't trust her in equal measure.

"You're one of the good ones," she said simply. "I trust you." She looked at the money again. With her index finger, she touched each bill and counted aloud: 20, 40, 60 ....

I stopped her at 220. "What'll you buy first?" I asked.

She considered. "A ticket. Then something with mink."

"Okay, a ticket. You'll have to steal a couple hundred more for the mink, though."

She shrugged. She didn't allow me to prick her fantasy, not like that. "A beautiful display, ain't it? Say one of your French things about it."

I laughed. "You remember that?"

"Naturally," she said.

There was a time when I'd affected a French accent during my act, using it on clients susceptible to such things. I peppered my speech with French phrases, residue from childhood lessons my grandfather forced on me. Foreignness had a lot of mileage in that business, especially with hicks who never saw Paris.

"Rouler sur l'or," I said. My French was unpracticed, badly in need of greasing, just awkward phrases these days. *Rolling in money*, this one meant. Something like that. I passed my hand over the cash to add some theater.

Anna liked that.

The cash was beautiful in the same way a cupboard of food is beautiful to the hungry. So, yes, it was a beautiful array. The bills reminded me of something else, too. A vivid image came to me, something I hadn't thought about in years.

"You remember the old joke about doing a séance with King Death?" I said. It was a tired vaudeville sketch. Anna had to remember it, it was so ubiquitous on the circuit (especially with the fools who'd been hustling since the twenties), but the gin made me want to talk. "Where the swami reaches out to the Grim Reaper because everybody in the room wants to know when they'll die. So the swami asks for everybody's expiration dates."

Anna furrowed her brow and looked puzzled. "I must've missed that one, old boy."

"No, no. You remember. It was old even in the forties." She couldn't have been on the circuit and not seen it. I'd seen it multiple times as part of what were called Spook Shows, travelling acts that did a slate of sketches, magic acts, séances, and showed black and white horror pictures to cap the night.

Anna shook her head.

"The swami gets King Death on the line, right, and—" It wasn't appropriate now, not with the look on Anna's face. Maybe she'd gone batty and thought such a thing portentous.

Coincidence or portents was an old saying we used in those days. When on top, everything is coincidence. When sinking, portents.

Anna wouldn't have been the first to fall for her own flimflam. I tried to drop it because it wasn't funny anyhow. It was just an old image in a sleep-deprived brain.

"—And what?"

We stared at each other for a moment.

I broke. "Well," I finished lamely, "you know the rest. Sometimes people do the skit with a crystal ball and sometimes with tarot cards. It's just the money reminds me of cards, the way you laid it out." I'd seen, in fact, a couple septuagenarians do the act with dollar bills in place of tarot.

"No, I wanna hear it," Anna persisted.

Then I knew that she remembered the skit as well as I did.

She thought I was being righteous, condemning the money, which was far from the truth.

An edge crept into her voice. "I wanna laugh."

"You have any cigarettes in your purse?" I asked. I wasn't having any of her games. Anna didn't intimidate me, gun moll grin or not. She was the one needing help. She was the one in trouble.

Poised over the money, she shook her head. "Well, what's the punch line, Royce?"

"Okay, if you're not going to let it drop. Fine. The Reaper picks up the telephone and these two, he and the swami, get to talking. They make small talk about weather and traffic, and then the swami asks the question: I have clients here who want to know when they'll croak. Death gets to sweating and wiping his brow because he doesn't know the answer to that. He's just a fry cook who takes orders. But the swami thinks he'll know, and King Death doesn't want to disappoint admirers. 'Well?' the swami asks. Death scrambles and says, 'Ten minutes.' 'Why ten minutes?' At that point Death breaks the connection. The swami tells his clients you're going to be dead in ten minutes. 'All of us?' 'That's what he said.' And then, ten minutes later everybody, save for the swami, croaks. A minute after that the phone rings. It's Death again. The swami, puzzled, says, 'Death, why ten minutes?' Wicked King Death says, 'Traffic.'"

Anna stared at me.

"King Death had to save face, so he killed them. He would've done it instantly if there wasn't traffic."

"How the hell is that supposed to be funny?"

"It isn't, but you didn't help the timing. A receptive audience makes a difference."

"What's the moral?"

"Don't analyze it, dear."

"What's it supposed to mean?"

"Don't meddle. Don't tempt fate."

Anna stacked the bills and folded the wad. The money disappeared into her purse again. That was that.

I fooled around, straightening a magazine, until the silence passed.

Finally, Anna slid closer. She eased in until her warmth reached me. "Maybe you just aren't funny," she said.

"Fair enough. You sure you don't have a loose cigarette in that thing?"

"I've looked it over twice. I'm sure."

"A mint?"

"I'm not your granny, old boy."

I cursed myself for not buying more cigarettes before leaving The Sherwood.

Anna sidled against me.

"You look just like Mina in *Dracula*," I said. "After she's bitten and when she's sultry. When she has the wrap around her neck. Anybody ever tell you that?"

"Never saw it."

"It was twenty feet tall in front of your face tonight. Same eyes. Same hair."

Anna was an inch from my face. "I noticed you didn't try anything on me in the bedroom," she said. "Most men would've tried something." She placed her hand on my leg, moved it up my thigh. "Why not? You still a fairy, Royce? You still bat that way?"

What a question.

"Mansfield didn't change the fact, if that's how you mean."

Anna smirked. "From the stories I hear, jail probably strengthened it."

I shrugged.

"You can't change back and forth?"

I laughed. "If only."

The simple woman waited, unsatisfied.

"No, it doesn't work like that," I said.

"So you'd just as soon stick it in that bottle than a woman, I suppose. My mouth works like any other mouth, you know, if not better."

"I'm sure it does, dear, but you're selling me short. It isn't like that."

Anna snorted and backed off. "I was just curious," she said. "I need it a little. It helps me sleep."

"You wouldn't give it up even if I wanted it," I said.

She considered, and the pause made me wonder. "Probably not."

That got us both laughing.

I like to think back and imagine where the night would've gone if nothing else occurred in those small hours. We would've finished the bottle, and we would've talked more. We would've tried to convince each other about things. There's really no telling, but it would've been pleasant, even if insincere.

Of course, that didn't happen.

A knock came at the door, perhaps the worst sound in the world, and then all hell broke loose.

CHAPTER FOUR

Anna's blood drained. She was a ghost again, as pale as when she came running into the Marley Caldwell. Before the third knock fell, she asked, "Where do you keep your gun?" Her mind went there immediately.

I fought to remain level.

The door rattled with the persistent knocking. Then the hoarse voice of Wendell Marsh came through the wood.

"Anna!" he shouted. "Anna, you in there?"

He tried the door, but it didn't give. I'd locked it twice over, and the slab was made of heavy material. His fist landed again, shaking the room. The sound went through me. The sound sobered me.

"Goddamnit, Anna, you bitch! Anna!"

I jumped to my feet. I'd freeze in place if I didn't move. That was something I'd learned at a young age. Everything depends on those first seconds, so I moved despite the terror.

I didn't keep a gun, in fact. I told Anna so. Convicts can't buy guns legally, and I wasn't interested in getting one by the other method. I kept the blackjack for my walks on East 14th, though. I grabbed my usher jacket and pulled the small weapon from the inner pocket. It was a leather sap no longer than an outstretched hand, and it held a fat metal rod inside. It was a sap cops used when breaking skulls.

"Where did he see us?" Anna whispered, confused.

"Anywhere. Didn't have to be him," I said. "But somebody was following you."

The knocking made it impossible to think. I considered going out the window and down the fire escape. Like a fool, I even considered switching off the lamp and hiding in the bedroom. Thankfully, the mania passed and better judgment prevailed.

Anna stood from the couch. She looked at the blackjack and shook her head disapprovingly. She grew more poised now, which worried me. She wasn't scared in the same way I was scared. She reached to her purse and pulled out a small pistol.

Oh hell, I thought.

She fished a bullet and loaded the thing with familiarity. It was a Beretta, and it fit her hand nicely. A mouse gun, yet enough to kill when used properly. Anna was educated on the matter. She aimed the muzzle at the shaking door.

I heard more voices. Other people gathered in the hallway. That was inevitable. Marsh was too loud to escape attention. Mrs. Kohut would be up to the fourth floor soon. She'd call the police. I hoped Marsh would give it up and run. My hand sweated around the sap, uncertain.

Marsh stopped for a beat of silence, like he was taking a deep breath, and then the door crashed inward, splintering along the frame. With tremendous force, he'd kicked it open with one blow. He kicked once more to finish the job, and the door flung wide. There he stood like a lunatic on speed. He wasn't a tall man, a couple inches shorter than me, but he was muscular and stout. His neck was wider than his ears, and his face was pocked and scarred. He was high on something.

His eyes went from Anna to me and then Anna again.

"You bitch," he slurred. His chest heaved. He saw the gun in her steady hand. The sight locked him in place.

At the same time, my waking dream surfaced, and I saw Barnett standing before me in the courtyard at Mansfield. I'd thought a lot about what I'd do if I ever caught Barnett vulnerable. That image put a charge in me.

In Marsh's second of hesitation, I rushed him with the blackjack.

It was movement accomplished with little thought. I may not be much with my hands but given a weapon I can take down anyone. I had a good stomach for blood. Just as Marsh brought up his fist, I swung the rod in an upward arc, like backhanding a tennis racket. The sap caught his chin, metal on bone. The punch he started went nowhere, softening as his muscles quit. Marsh's head snapped back with a crack. I kept my momentum and shoved his arm aside with my free hand and then brought the blackjack down again, this time hard against the side of his neck. The blow doubled him over, but it didn't take him down. He spat blood. He came back with a swing that caught nothing except air.

Anna rushed forward with the pistol.

Marsh blocked my next swing, and he tackled me to the ground. The whole apartment quaked. If he got on top of me, it would be over. He'd beat my head in like a rotten gourd, and Anna would have to save me with the gun. With luck and good timing, I managed to get higher than Marsh, freeing my shoulders. His face was down, parallel with the floor, so I smacked the rod against the back of his skull. It landed with a sickening thud, splitting the skin under his hair. Blood made a sopping mess, running over his left ear and down his face. It ran as fast as his heart. I hit Marsh again. I shouldn't have done that, but I couldn't control myself. He didn't put up a defense, so the second strike landed even harder than the first.

He went down, prostrate against the floor.

Marsh groaned, barely conscious. The damage to his head made him piss all over the rug on which he lay. A puddle spread beneath his body. I thought he was brain dead. He didn't do anything else. He just groaned.

"Let me finish it," Anna said coldly.

I looked up at her. My fist still buzzed and there was blood on it. I was short of breath. I wanted her to finish it, but I argued with myself.

She knelt and placed the muzzle behind Marsh's ear. He didn't protest. His eyes darted like eyes do with seizures.

Gently, slowly, I wrapped my hand around Anna's wrist.

"Don't," I managed to say, breathing heavily. I nodded over my shoulder.

A few people I didn't know, along with a couple I did, peered in from the hallway. They were wide-eyed, dumb with the heat of the moment. None of them moved to help.

I lifted Anna's hand until a sliver of light separated Marsh's hair and the muzzle. Anna did the rest. She put the gun away.

She looked at me and said, "We gotta leave, Royce."

"It was self-defense. We got witnesses. It's on him, not us."

She shook her head tightly. Her eyes said there was more to the story.

"What didn't you tell me?" I asked. I looked down at Marsh. He didn't have a gun, I noticed. He was groaning, still conscious.

"We just gotta leave," she repeated. "We gotta leave *now*."

I cleaned my sap on the rug. That gave me a couple seconds to think things over, and I did my best. A lot of pent up feelings prodded me. Anna retrieved her shoes and purse, while I threw a few belongings in a soiled laundry bag, and then we were stepping over Marsh and heading out the door. Mrs. Kohut, decked in a robe and curlers, saw me on the stairwell and shouted something about rent and damages. I don't think she'd seen Marsh at that point. Or her rug. I shouted something I shouldn't have (she was an old lady, after all), but it felt pretty damn good.

Outside, the cold air braced me. The sun had yet to rise, and the streets were dark. I ran after Anna. She'd gone ahead, running for her life. It's hard to explain the exhilaration of that moment. This was the height of things. For a few minutes, I was a lunatic, but I was free. We even got to laughing as we ran, and that noise was up and down the street, echoing.

CHAPTER FIVE

It took an entire pack of Chesterfields to bring me down
a notch. With a loan from Anna, I bought that pack and
a couple more at a drugstore in the Greyhound depot. The
clerk was asleep on his feet. He didn't mind that I looked like
a junkie with rust-colored blood on my hands. He told me to
have a nice day.

While Anna cleaned up in the restroom, I chain-smoked
and watched people. A small crowd shuffled about the ter-
razzo floors of the station. A few people hauled luggage, while
most carried nothing more than a newspaper. The space was
as cold as a cave, and the tall ceiling produced echoes. The
aromas of coffee and exhaust mingled. I scanned each corner for the Queen City constabulary, but no patrolmen were
about, not yet.

There weren't many options for leaving Cincinnati at five
in the morning. Most of the available buses were intercity, run
by the transit authority, whereas Greyhound buses were in the
process of arriving rather than departing. Anna and I scanned
the board. The cold got to me. My knees knocked. Anna had
my coat, and I only had the sweatshirt. I'd left the usher jacket
behind. Although Columbus and Dayton were options, we
agreed that leaving Ohio was best. Crossing the state line

gave us the semblance of protection. It would, if nothing else, complicate things for authorities. Chicago was an option if we waited until eight, but we couldn't afford three more hours in Cincinnati.

"How about this one?" Anna asked.

She pointed to a 5:10 departure for a place named Huntington. It was in West Virginia, and the fare was cheap. A hick town. I didn't have much love for hick towns or people across the river in Kentucky, and I assumed I wouldn't feel differently about West Virginia. Both states had reputations. Cincinnati, in many ways, is a frontier, the southern boundary of civilization. Once you cross the line southward you enter the Bible Belt. That was another world. Down there they accused everyone of being communist or atheist. God forbid you were Black on that soil. Kentucky gas stations still sold postcards to commemorate lynchings. I'd seen them.

I kept my feelings about Huntington to myself.

A map behind glass on the wall showed all the bus routes. It was a spider web of red, green, and blue. I found Huntington without much searching. It was up river about 100 miles distant, and it bordered Ohio. I showed Anna.

"Good enough?" she asked.

I agreed. *We can make for Pittsburgh afterward*, I thought, *if Huntington doesn't work. We can dip a foot in the South and then run back North.*

Once we'd purchased tickets, we boarded an idling Greyhound. No one stopped us. The fear that someone would intervene stayed in the back of my mind. I found no cops standing on the concrete platform.

The bus was a newer model and clean, especially in contrast to the intercity buses waiting nearby. Anna and I found open seats despite the dark interior. The coach was fairly empty. We shoved our belongings under the seats before us. No one sat there and no one sat behind us. It was all very simple, inconspicuous, and mundane. No one gave a side-eyed glance. All this had me worrying about the lack of friction, but I was being paranoid.

Anna watched the window as we pulled out of the station. The simple thrust of changing gears brought a swell of relief.

"You really got him good," Anna said. "Really good, old boy."

She was reliving the moment with Marsh. She liked watching someone beat on him for a change.

"He pissed himself." She smiled. "Think it'll make the paper?"

"Marsh pissing his pants?"

She made a face.

I dismissed that. "Not a chance," I said. "He's nobody."

I didn't want to think about Marsh dying. *He'll live,* I convinced myself. Wendell Marsh was too stupid and mean to die so easily. *But what if he doesn't die? Then what? I got lucky with that first hit. What would he do?* I didn't want to explore those things, but the thoughts paraded through my mind, regardless.

Anna grabbed my hand. "My hero," she said, and laughed a small laugh that suited the darkness. "Royce Pembrook, the toughest fairy I know."

"Don't say that." I was used to that type of ribbing. I shouldn't have been used to it, but I was. Still, I didn't like that she was doing it here and now. Other people would hear.

"How'd you learn to use a sap like that?" she whispered.

I pulled away. "Just lay off it," I said.

"Was it in prison?"

I rolled my eyes, but the gesture was lost in the low light.

"You must have big ideas about me," I said. "You read too much *Manhunt* and *Prison Confessions*. I learned it from movies, as a matter of fact."

"Is that right?" She thought I was being facetious.

Partially, I thought.

A beat of silence passed. The city rushed by. The engine whirred.

"Were you going to shoot Marsh?" I asked.

Anna still had the Beretta with her. She shrugged off the question. I watched her, but she wasn't looking at me anymore. Her eyes went back to the window, where the Ohio River came into view. The river's surface was dark and oily. The horizon showed the purple tinge of first light.

"It's snowing," she muttered. "Crazy weather."

Indeed, flurries fell over the water. It was much too early in the season for that. It was only October, after all.

If we keep heading south, we'll end up where it's hot all the time, I thought. That consoled me. I wanted to be someplace warm, and I wanted to stay there for good. I folded my arms.

We were both asleep before the Greyhound hit Route 52 and followed the river southward.

CHAPTER SIX

Huntington was a middling town full of steel mills, traffic, and railroad tracks. Perched on the Ohio River, and encased with brick, it boasted a handful of ten story buildings and no skyline. Noxious smoke dirtied the air. It was a busy, sprawling town with the pretense of being Pittsburgh. Without the size or anything remotely cosmopolitan, though, Huntington remained provincial. Unlike Pittsburgh, no Carnegie had lived and worked here.

Although only a tenth of Cincinnati's population, Huntington was large enough to house strangers and travelers without arousing suspicion. Hundreds of barges, trains, and buses passed through daily. Huntington was an artery through which a lot of stuff moved, but few things remained. It wasn't Main Street, USA. I'd had a worrying image of a more dire provincialism: elm trees, a single stop sign, and a diner where everybody turned their eyes when you stepped through the door.

The Greyhound deposited us at an art deco terminal at the intersection of Fourth Avenue and 13th Street. The depot had round edges with chrome trim and a sign with the eponymous canine over the entrance. It was brand new construction. A large parking lot stood in rear of the building, and a stone church loomed behind that, casting a shadow over the lot. No fleet of black and white patrol cars waited on us.

Be calm and stop thinking like that, I told myself. *If you keep looking for trouble, you'll find it.*

Anna and I went inside the station and found a diner with a slick counter and chrome-plated stools. The interior of the depot was pastel green and yellow with floors of narrow tile. Other travelers, of which there were few, moved hurriedly through the space, wading into the morning traffic on Fourth Avenue. The scent of fried bacon hung in the air. My stomach protested its neglect. The clock on the wall said it was early, only 8am. Anna and I sat at the counter. A mounted radio told us a station's call letters, WHTN, before the news proceeded. One of the nearby churches confirmed the clock with pealing bells.

I ordered the largest breakfast on the menu: a heaping plate of bacon, eggs, hash browns, tomatoes, toast, and coffee. Anna got a couple hardboiled eggs. I got lost in the aroma of the food when the man behind the counter set down the plate. He was an older gentleman who minded his business. He never said his name, and he never asked for our names. Rather than talking, he found things to clean, so I liked him fine. It was a good start.

Around the edge of a mouthful, I told Anna she'd made a decent choice.

She grabbed a saltshaker and smiled wryly.

"What's that look for?" I asked.

She shrugged. "Might be we didn't land here by chance alone," she said.

A middle-aged woman and two boys tock seats at the counter. They'd been on the same Greyhound as us. I felt the children staring at me, but I didn't look over. To hell with kids. They were amoral shits.

I shoveled in more food and then washed it down. "How about telling me the truth then?"

"About everything?" She shook her head. "Tsk tsk." She picked at her egg.

It didn't feel like a joke to me. "Just this about Huntington would be okay for now." Anna owed me the truth. *Why lie about a thing like that?*

"Don't boil over, old boy. It's just this: we woulda been at the station at five whether Wendell chased us out or not. I'd planned that far. And I'd planned to come here. He or his friends was after me, so I came to you first." She touched my hand playfully. It was greasy. "Naturally, you were a darling. A hero."

I put down my fork. "Why this place?"

Anna nibbled at the egg with her front teeth. I was reminded of a cat teasing a sinew of meat. It wasn't alluring.

"I know somebody here that can help us out," she said. "It's simple as that. I didn't tell you because it didn't seem advantageous at the time to tell you. So what? Call me troubled."

"It's a silly thing to lie about is all."

"If you want an apology, you can forget it. You and I can make a little money with this guy, and then, if you want, you can go your own way. I might go to Pittsburgh," she added. "How about you?"

I took another bite. I recalled why I hadn't missed Anna in the years she'd been absent from my life. She had a maddening, grating way. I kept the peace and moved on. "Can't go back to Cincinnati," I commented. That truth made me think about Mr. Pedersoli.

God, he'll be sore when I don't show for work tonight. Poor Mrs. Pedersoli.

"No," she agreed, "you can't. I did you a favor with that. You can close that chapter."

"I might head out to Phoenix," I said, "where it's warm. Out West." That wasn't exactly well thought out. Phoenix had occurred to me in a dream on the bus, I realized. The dream came from all those ads in magazines about traveling by plane. Yet the dream suited me, and the desire felt like one I'd always possessed. There was something organic about its surfacing here and now. I had nothing positive anchoring me to the East. Why not shake it up?

Anna raised her eyebrows, surprised. "That's a long haul," she said. The West didn't exist to her and, honestly, it hadn't existed for me until now. We'd been confined to dirty river cities our entire lives. Pittsburgh was exotic to us. I wondered why I moved back to Cincinnati after Mansfield. It was a question I couldn't answer.

No more, I thought. *No more of these grimy towns. Now it's Phoenix.*

Anna continued shaving the egg with her little teeth, finally exposing the yolk.

"We can make some money how?" I asked.

"Remember when I asked if you missed the business?"

"Goddamn it."

"Royce, you're good at it. You got talent. I saw the way you talked about it. You *do* miss it."

I pushed around the food on my plate. When it came to scamming and conning people, I had too much talent. That was precisely why I was trying to stay out of the field. One foot back into that world and I'd be addicted. Truthfully, I felt the pull already.

At that moment, two city cops in dark uniforms walked through the front entrance of the depot. The crowd from the last two buses had departed, so the cops stood out. They were young men, slender, with flat top haircuts. Beat cops on patrol. They looked like war vets. With bright sunlight at their backs, the men stood just within the twin doors. They gazed around, scanning the station.

I eyed Anna and offered a quick prayer over my food. Anna clammed up and concentrated on her egg.

The cops moved toward the restaurant counter and talked to the old man in low tones. I hoped they'd all laugh, but that didn't happen. With dour expressions, the cops walked around and sat on the stools directly beside me.

My nerves burned. Tension spread through my body.

The cop nearest, a bruiser with corded neck and arms, looked at my unfinished plate. "Eyes bigger than your stomach," he said.

The old man placed two mugs and filled each with drip coffee. The cops took the coffee black.

"The smell got me," I said. I nodded at the old man. "He should've stopped me."

The old man turned his back without saying anything. He didn't smile or laugh. I liked how he didn't give a damn. I admired that.

With smug and phony politeness, the cop smiled. His buddy worked on the coffee, sipping loudly, but the deputy nearest remained interested in Anna and me. He didn't like what he saw. He let his coffee steam and said, "I got intuition about people, fellah. That's what makes me good at what I do."

You and me and the devil makes three.

Goddamn it, I hate cops. They're bullies, all of them. My

appetite died. I pushed around the food some more, mainly the greasy meat. The pork. A live pig next to a dead pig.

Don't break out in a sweat, I willed.

From my pocket, I pulled a pack of Chesterfields. I took one out, fished a match from a pot on the counter, and lit the cigarette. I offered one to Anna, which she declined, but I didn't offer one to the cop. The first hit did wonders. I exhaled through my nose and smoke spread over my plate.

"You look like a good cop," I agreed. "An upstanding young citizen."

His partner laughed as if he knew something I didn't.

The cop tested his coffee, frowned, and asked, "What brings you folks here? And I'll rock your world, buddy, if you say the good folks at Greyhound."

Anna took over to keep me from being smart. "We're here to visit an old friend, officer." She smiled and, to my surprise, it was charming, genuine.

"Uh-huh. And who would that be?" the cop asked.

"Ruben Graf," Anna said.

That was news to me just like it was news to the cop. I didn't know a Ruben Graf. I'd remember a name like that.

Adroitly, the cop observed, "That's a kraut name."

His partner spoke finally. "Lay off it, Jimmy," he muttered. "I have a kraut name. You know I don't like when you talk like that."

"Still. A lot of those Nazis escaped," Jimmy said. "You never know."

The officer chewed his lip and then tried his coffee again. Either his imagination failed him or he grew bored with the exchange.

Thank God he doesn't have us alone in an alley, and thank

God we aren't Black, I thought. Jimmy could give me a lesson on how to wield a sap.

After a moment, he said, "We don't allow vagrancy in this town. Do you understand that? No panhandling. No loitering period. At all."

"We're just tired, officer," Anna said coolly. "We're not homeless."

The cop nodded. He finished his coffee. "I don't wanna see you again," Jimmy said.

I nodded. That much was mutual.

Anna and I waited out the officers. When the cops left, we pushed away our plates and paid the tab. We didn't want Jimmy to get sordid ideas about us paying with fresh money, so we waited until he was out of sight. Seeing Anna's wad of twenties was all Jimmy the Cop needed.

The man behind the counter spoke to us for the first time. "Jimmy's a prick," he observed. "He was a prick when he was a kid, and he's a prick now. Prick kids become prick adults. Pig bastards."

I thought that was philosophical.

The old man winked at Anna when she slipped him the change as a tip.

CHAPTER SEVEN

Who's Ruben Graf?" I asked.

Anna and I walked the sidewalk. It was cold, but the sky was blue and the sun was out. The street was a corridor of shops: barbers, beauty parlors, bookstores, clothing boutiques, and a few bars. Foot traffic was light, while the street was hectic with bulky sedans and trucks. A breeze whipped through the trees on Fourth Avenue, buffeting the shop awnings that edged the curb. The trees weren't quite dead yet, although the colorful leaves fell rapidly, blanketing the sidewalk. To little avail, the shop owners tackled the debris with brooms.

Anna shielded her face from the wind. "We're going to meet Ruben now," she said. "He's expecting me."

Me, not us, I thought.

After taking a left up to Sixth Avenue, we walked four blocks through the shadow of churches, row houses, and offices to 9th Street. Once there, Anna stared across the two-way street at a building tall enough to be a skyscraper in this town. It stood thirteen stories and tapered to a slender edge. I shaded my eyes, looking up. I hadn't seen many architectural flourishes since arriving, but here one stood. The sign on the top read *Hotel Prichard.* The buff colored brick and stone building was very fine once, perhaps in the 1920s, and the restaurant on its ground floor had been chic. Although wilted now, and in need of a facelift, the building possessed an air of finery, and the restaurant remained out of my price range.

"This is too nice," I said. "Unless you're paying."

"Ruben does well, don't he?" Anna said.

I bit my tongue. Doing well in our business isn't the sign of a good man.

We crossed the street. A sandwich board under the front canopy boasted about J. Fredd Muggs, a chimpanzee from television, who had stayed in one of the hotel's three hundred rooms. *Hell of an advertisement.*

I wasn't confident we were dressed to enter. I wore my sweatshirt from the night prior, and I carried a stained laundry bag. Anna's clothes were a step up, but the oversized coat gave her the appearance of a bag lady.

I discarded my cigarette. "I'll wait outside and smoke another."

Anna yanked me by the arm.

"Just one telephone call and we'll be seeing Jimmy again," I warned.

"Jimmy can go play in traffic," Anna said.

We walked in. Fine marble and walnut decorated the spacious lobby. I peered toward the restaurant. The room had a domed ceiling replete with gold leaf. A touch of class always had an impact on me. It drew me, and I loved class as much as I hated tacky poverty. Marble made me think of my old days with Fawn Bailey, about how one of those heiresses could have you living very well if she admired you. I contrasted that lifestyle with my current predicament. The disparity gnawed at me.

Anna stepped up to the desk and clerk. I stood at her side, ashamed.

The clerk, a young man with hair greased back and dewy skin, quite pretty, looked at us like we were about to beg him for a nickel. He was prepared to snarl. I watched his lip quiver, fighting it. I hated myself for that, not him. I understood the sentiment.

"We're here to meet Mr. Ruben Graf," Anna said. "He's expecting us."

The clerk pretended to be confounded, racking his memory for names.

Anna stared until he gave up the act.

"Mr. Graf didn't mention visitors," the clerk said.

"Oh, come off it. Does he usually?"

The clerk admitted that Graf did not.

"We need to see him *now*," Anna said. "Take us up or bring him down."

"You'll have to be escorted." He looked at me when he said that.

I smiled at him. His eyes softened. We locked for a moment and shared a little tension.

I knew it. What's it like to be a gay man in West Virginia? I thought. *A true nightmare. If I ever get him alone, I'll ask him.* I planned on getting him alone. It had been a few months for me.

"We clean up well," I promised.

He passed it all off. I understood the deflection. It meant nothing.

"I'm sure you do, sir, but—"

"—Take us up then," Anna interjected. "*Now*." She split her gaze between the two of us. She gripped her purse until her knuckles whitened.

Flustered, the clerk agreed. He dinged his bell, and a boy emerged from what I'd assumed to be a broom closet. He straightened his jacket and moved toward the desk.

"Hiya, folks," he said. "Right this way."

I smiled at the clerk again, and I let it linger.

. . .

The kid took us to the tenth floor in an elevator. When the doors split, we stepped out, and I asked him if J. Fredd Muggs, the chimp, had stayed on this floor. The kid thought that was ludicrous, but he offered to tell me who *had* stayed on this floor in 1949. Apparently, there were so few celebrities in Huntington that you could mark the year by their visit.

"Mr. Gene Autry, star of stage, radio, and screen." He pointed to a suite.

Anna rolled her eyes.

I whistled admiration. "Impressive," I said.

The kid agreed that it was impressive.

"Where'd his horse stay? In the same room as the chimp?"

"Champion?" The kid shrugged. "I don't know. Did you know he had more than one horse named Champion?"

"I didn't," I admitted.

We stopped when we reached the end of the corridor. He led us to the last door on the right.

"Mr. Graf makes this his residence," he whispered. "Quite a few folks choose to live here. We try to grant him privacy." He knocked softly and leaned his ear toward the wood. "Mr. Graf? Mr. Graf, will you accept visitors?"

Whoever Graf was, he garnered a bit of respect from the kid. Of course, that meant money and generosity.

A beat of silence passed. Shuffling followed. Then a man's

voice issued from behind the door. The sleep in his voice reminded me that it was still early. The hours were mixed in my mind. Last night still hadn't ended as far as I was concerned.

Graf didn't open the door. "Who is it?" he asked.

The kid looked at us.

"It's Anna."

I didn't say anything. He wouldn't know me from Adam.

The bolt slid and the chain jingled. The door opened to reveal a man in his fifties, dressed in silk pajamas. An RG monogram decorated the chest. Money or not, I recognized his type. It was an instant feeling. He was a chiseler who struck gold. He'd risen, as it were. However he'd done it, he'd done it, and it didn't make anyone glad for his achievement. He had pale blue eyes and touches of white in his blond hair. Although I wouldn't call him handsome, he had an inoffensive face that one could trust. Plainness was his asset. I had the feeling his features allowed him to change identity as needed from time to time.

Graf looked at Anna with a smile and looked at me with flat nothing, and then he told the kid to get moving.

I gave the kid a dime from my cigarette change.

"Who's this?" Graf asked. His voice was hard, somewhat graveled. He nodded at me.

"Ruben, this is Royce Pembrook. Royce, this is Ruben Graf."

I shook his hand. It was dry. He squeezed the bones to show he was a man.

Anna went on before Graf protested. "I wouldn't be here now if it weren't for Royce."

I doubted that. I thought about Anna and her gun.

"I've mentioned him to you before. He was the one who had Fawn Bailey on the line before us."

Graf looked at me, and, as he did, a memory clicked into place. I had the odd feeling that I was watching choreography unfold. I couldn't put my finger on it, but the scene felt practiced.

"That's right," he said. He snapped his fingers. "Yeah, okay. Mrs. Bailey still likes you, you know? She said you looked like Conrad Veidt."

Veidt was a sophisticated look, at least. She'd told me several times that I resembled the German actor.

"It's my pitiful hairline," I joked. *And the gauntness, perhaps.* Food was pretty expensive the last few months. I resembled Conrad Veidt, but it was a reference for grandmothers, lost on most.

Graf laughed. You can't go wrong with self-deprecation around a man like him. In that moment, I read Graf. In my own way, I knew him, and I knew what he wanted to hear. I knew him well enough to get an awful vibe from him. I didn't know him well enough to expect what happened next.

Anna slid into his open arms and gave him a deep kiss.

Graf forgot all about me. I stood like a creep, watching, unsure what to do. Finally, Anna stopped and pulled a twenty from her purse. She handed over the cash.

"Get a room and get cleaned up," she ordered.

Graf nodded at me, offered a smarmy wink, and then he pulled Anna inside the room. The door shut, leaving me alone in the corridor. Anna giggled from the other side. Sun came through the window at my left.

I looked at the twenty in my hands and wondered what Wendell Marsh would think about this. I held his money, while Graf held his girl and his money and whatever else.

To put it mildly, he'd be displeased, I thought. *Irked.*

I had an opportunity to rush back to the bus depot and

start westward toward Phoenix. No one would stop me, but I didn't even consider it. I wanted more of the thing I held in my hand. It was as simple as that. I ignored my gut. I called the elevator. I had the intention of getting a room, and possibly more, from the pretty clerk in the lobby.

Dominic, the golden tag on his uniform read.

CHAPTER EIGHT

Seized from a fever dream, I awoke. I was in the middle of a hell of a nightmare. For a few seconds, confusion reigned. Blood pulsed. Sweat beaded. Stigmas blurred my eyes. I was in an unfamiliar room. I sat up in an unfamiliar bed, convinced I was trapped. Pressure bore down on me like the metal jaws of a vise.

The door of my room rattled under the weight of an insistent fist. That was real. Three bursts and a pause. The door moved. Three bursts and a breath.

Wendell Marsh, I thought, and true terror went through me. *I should've let Anna kill him. We should've had it over and done with that night.*

In a moment of clarity, I realized Marsh had been in the dream.

A dream, I thought. I took a breath and gathered myself. *You're not in Cincinnati. It was a dream.* I repeated that until I braced myself and stood.

I shuffled across the carpet to the door. Plucking up the courage, I asked, "What do you want?" My breath was heavy like I'd sprinted the distance.

The knocking stopped. A beat of silence followed.

"What do you want?" I repeated.

"Are you kidding?" It was Anna's voice. "Christ, Royce, open the door."

Not without caution, I unlocked the door and pulled it inward.

Anna stood alone on the other side of the threshold. My coat draped her arm. "What's wrong with you? I was knockin' for five minutes. I thought I'd have to call a medic."

I poked my head out and surveyed the hall. A man and a child stood at the far end, but otherwise Anna was alone. I searched for Marsh.

"You're all grey," she said.

I rubbed my head. "I feel like a husk." The knocking was gone, but my head throbbed with the rhythm of it.

Anna shoved the coat toward me, moved me aside, and entered the room. I shut the door, and then I hung the coat on a hook. The fabric looked even rattier than it had before. I turned to find Anna with her hands on her hips, looking around the room admiringly. She wore new clothes.

How long was I out? I thought.

She wore a fine-looking broadcloth jacket and skirt, mustard yellow and fitted to show her slender figure. Faux mink lined the collar and cuffs. Graf stopped short of draping her in real mink. Okay, so he wasn't rich. Still, Anna's transformation impressed me. Graf did more for Anna than a hood like Marsh could do.

After taking in the room, she turned her feline eyes back on me.

I went to the nightstand and got a Chesterfield. The first taste of smoke eased the throbbing in my skull. I crossed an arm over my stomach and rested the elbow of my other arm on top of it.

"Too bad you couldn't get a room on the tenth floor," Anna said. "They're bigger. They're suites."

I'd requested a room from Dominic that was *not* on the tenth floor. Common sense guided that decision. Distance is a good bedfellow for uncertainty, and I was uncertain about plenty.

She moved to the window with grace. I hardly recognized her as the woman nibbling an egg at the Greyhound depot. Both of us were good at transformations, though. Anna pushed aside the heavy curtains, and the sun spread across the floor. Dust moved in the shaft of light.

Looking out, she said, "Not quite the view you get on the tenth."

That was the one too many. My decision didn't set right with her, I realized. She knew I didn't trust her. Skepticism got under her skin.

I smoked some more before joining Anna. Finally, when I did, I said, "The seventh was all Dominic had. It's a busy place. Maybe there's a show in town."

She laughed at the thought.

"Gene Autry was here seven years ago. The singing cowboy."

"Dominic? The two of you on a first name basis now?"

I shrugged. "I'm trying."

"I don't blame you. He's a beauty. What'd he say to you?"

"Not enough, but I'll keep at it." I looked her up and down. "I need new threads."

"Why? Is he shallow?"

"I'm shallow," I said.

We looked out at the streets of Huntington: bricks, autumn leaves, a few pedestrians, a few cars.

"What view are you talking about?" I asked. "Is there a lake and sailboats on the other side? Or is it more of this?"

"You can see all the way to the river up there."

I stepped from the window. "I can do without the sludge river. I've seen enough of it."

She lost some of her elegance when she took the cigarette from my hand and put it in her mouth. She worked on it too quickly. She might as well bite her knuckles.

"Why are you crabby?" she asked.

I shrugged, feeling irritable now that she suggested it. "How long did I sleep?"

"Four or five hours."

I didn't expect that. It felt like thirty minutes. "Will you sit down and let me ask you something?" I said.

Anna was agreeable. She went to a desk and turned the seat around. There wasn't much furniture in the room, just bare basics: a bed, a couple chairs, a table, desk, dresser, lamp, no telephone, and a cramped bathroom. The carpet was thick and expensive a decade prior. Now you could construct a new human from all the skin in it.

"Ask away," Anna said.

I sat on the edge of the bed. The frame was brass. The weakened bolts groaned.

"Why don't you tell me more about Graf?" I asked.

"Don't tell me you're jealous, old boy."

I gave her a look and laughed, and I imagine she regarded that as unkind. So be it. I was, as she observed, irritable.

"I want to know what I'm getting into. You have me paranoid as hell that Marsh is going to show at my door and break my neck. That's not your fault, but the least you can do is be straight with me. I risked a lot for you."

She finished my cigarette and found one of several glass ashtrays that dotted the room.

"Wendell didn't make the papers," she said.

"He wouldn't in this town. You think more of him than the rest of the world."

She shook her head. "Ruben gets the *Cincinnati Enquirer* brought up. They got that, Columbus, and Pittsburgh in the lobby. I scanned through it and there wasn't nothin'."

"Why would that relax me? That just means he isn't dead. If they'd even report a hood like him being knocked off, which I doubt. Read it tomorrow and see if it says the same."

"I planned on it. I'll be sure to send it down when I'm finished." Anna had a sardonic smile. She crossed her legs.

"Yeah, you do that. Now tell me about Graf."

"Another old flame," she said airily.

You're like a goddamn forest fire, I thought.

"I'm serious. I helped you, and I want to know."

After some fidgeting, she relented.

"Ruben has the market cornered here, and I knew he'd take us in. He's gotta couple guys that work for him, but he needs a couple more, and he's got a leash on every client in town. Savvy?"

I nodded. "Keep going," I said.

"There's a school here called Marshall. The faculty has a group that does séances. The president at the school is a real fanatic for it. He throws a lot of money at Ruben. Other than that, it's one-on-one stuff by appointment: fortune telling, palm reading, tarot, talking to dead relatives. Ruben will get you business, but he gets a cut. If you try to do it behind his back, he has a thug on the payroll to break bones." She paused, watching me. "Is that enough?"

I lit another cigarette. My headache eased more.

"How'd Graf end up in a shithole town like this?" I pointed the cigarette at Anna. The tip smoldered between my fingers. Ash lengthened. "That's the one thing I don't like. Nobody like him would choose to be here. It's too small of a pond. You told me he was in Cincinnati before."

"He was bigger than Cincy. He was big in Philly once, but then he did time in Eastern State. The two of you got that in common. Don't pry because I don't know any more about it. My guess is he wanted far away from that scene. He's laying low. He has a chance to be on top again here. I'd say he'll milk it and move on. It ain't permanent. Livin' in a hotel ain't permanent."

"How about you? You plan on sticking with him?"

"Now you're prying too much."

"Maybe."

"He'll be a good ally if Wendell shows," Anna said. "He's got ethics."

I chuckled. "Yeah, I know his kind of ethics."

"He'll get you enough work so that you can live here, live well, and pay for it on your own. He won't help you beyond that, and he'll kick you out before you get too popular. I won't lie. But you could do worse. You can build up a little cash and head toward Phoenix when you're done. I told Ruben that's what you wanted, and he didn't mind the idea. He ain't interested in handcuffin' you. No strings attached, old boy. What else do you expect? You really miss what you had goin' on yesterday?"

"Not particularly," I admitted. Footsteps and a rolling cart came and went in the hall. "It's just been a while."

"When you got talent you ain't gotta practice. You'll fall right into it." Anna stood. "Now get a bath and make yourself presentable. We're going out tonight. I imagine you could use a drink."

"A few," I said.

She looked me over. "You feel better now?"

Not really, I thought. I nodded, though, to appease Anna.

"Good boy," she said.

"You look fantastic."

"Don't I?" She took a step toward the door and then looked back at me over her shoulder. She needed a handbag to make it a pose from the pages of *Mademoiselle*.

CHAPTER NINE

We rode in style. Graf owned a two-toned Mercury Montclair coupe, polished teal and cream. The car had whitewall tires and a chrome M on the bonnet. The vehicle was brand new. The seats were stiff and made noise when you adjusted yourself. Graf babied the car at intersections, and he chastised me for attempting to smoke with the windows up. He kept the radio low so as not to burden the speakers. He cared for himself with the same level of attention: I watched his hands on the steering wheel and noticed they were freshly manicured. Everything was in place, everything perfect. In a sense, I was crashing a date and reunion between him and Anna. He was more than an old flame. The two melded too well. She was incapable of being completely honest, but sometimes she gave hints. She rested her head on his arm as he drove.

I was a third wheel and charity case, but that didn't stop me from enjoying the moment. I hadn't lived well in a while. I always enjoy nice things, new things. My grandfather, Wilhelm, made a fortune in the soda business, and he'd furnished a lavish life for me in childhood, so the desire to acquire and enjoy is in my blood. It's hard to escape. He was the last in the Pembrook line to have that money (the Depression, a couple ugly scandals with my mother, Eva, and the end of prohibition combined to wipe out his companies and investments), but he'd had it. I was alive when he had money, and that entrée doesn't leave your system. I'd seen London, Paris, Rome, and Seville, and I'd had expensive tutors. As the old song goes, "How you going to keep 'em down on the farm after they've seen Paree?"

I had a strong desire to do some work for Graf and buy new clothes. The ratty sport coat I'd brought along had busted seams, threadbare elbows, and wrinkles from being wadded in the laundry bag. The state of Ohio had given me the coat for job interviews when I'd left prison. They do that. There's even a handful of change and a dollar bill in your starter kit. I sometimes wondered if I was supposed to send back the coat when I was through with it. I'd worn it the first time I spoke to Mr. Pedersoli. Dinner tonight would be like a job interview, too, and I hoped it would be the last time I wore it.

Graf drove to a restaurant on Fourth Avenue called *Le Gros Raisin*. With a French name and menu, I thought it was bound to be empty, but the provincials liked the pretense of dressing up, eating a fancy meal, and then taking in a picture. Despite the bitter cold, Fourth Avenue was crowded. The restaurant stood on the same block as a striking movie palace called the Keith-Albee. Stepping out of Graf's Mercury, I admired the building from the sidewalk. It was an art deco relic of the 1930s, what the Marley Caldwell looked like when it had a more privileged clientele. Unlike Mr. Pedersoli's theater, though, this one was first run. This was the best in town whereas Mr. Pedersoli's wasn't even the tenth best in town. A sign like an Egyptian cartouche trimmed with fat light bulbs spelled out the theater's name vertically. It was just getting dark and the effect was lovely. The lights flashed on and off in a rhythm around the contour. A marquee with more light bulbs showed the name of tonight's picture: *The Ten Commandments.* A line of customers in heavy coats and hats started at the ticket booth and spread down the sidewalk. Mr. Pedersoli wouldn't get his hands on an expensive release like *The Ten Commandments* until January.

A French restaurant and Cecil B. DeMille, I thought, impressed. *Not a bad night.*

We entered *Le Gros Raisin* through a wooden door with a porthole. A crowd stood and waited in the foyer. Beyond this, the restaurant had low light and a solo violinist on a stage. Tables with candles covered the floor, and the tables were full. The violinist was struggling through a piece written for piano by Francis Poulenc. I assumed she and I had listened to the same concert on the radio a few months prior. How else Poulenc? He wasn't a name in the States. The girl wasn't particularly good, and the act wasn't particularly French, but a vague European air satisfied the locals. If there were candles, music, and foreign gibberish on the menu, it was worth the expense. The girl with a violin started into the strains of Stephen Foster's "Old Folks at Home" and suddenly I didn't feel sorry for her struggle anymore.

Graf bribed the maître d with a bill of which I didn't catch the denomination, and we moved to the front of the line. We followed a waiter to a table for four against the wall nearest the restrooms. A candle burned in a converted wine bottle at the center of the table. A cruet with garlic-infused olive oil stood in its halo of light. Prints of the Eiffel Tower and Arc de Triomphe on the wall above us offset the Greek touches. Anna and Graf sat on one side of the table, and I took the other.

Before opening a leather menu, Graf looked at me. He hadn't done that much, so there was gravity and meaning behind the stare. I had the feeling he was distinctly uncomfortable around me, although he was trying not to let it show. I couldn't tell if he was displeased by my presence or just wary of anyone new. He'd cut a rigid, somewhat stern figure thus far, so he took me by surprise when he made a joke.

"This is one of the three restaurants with tablecloths in town," he quipped. "Girls on roller skates bring food to your car in the others."

Although I was certain that was close to the truth, I laughed politely, just in case. If he wanted to make light, we'd make light. I'd planned on mirroring him until I got a feel of things. I still didn't know where I stood. "You know what *Le Gros Raisin* means?" I asked. I looked at Graf and then Anna.

"The nasty raisin," Anna said, matter-of-factly. "And it doesn't sound remotely appetizing. Le means The."

Graf shrugged.

"The Fat Grape," I answered.

"Look at you, Mr. Quiz Show," Anna said. She smiled at Graf, as if they were sharing a joke, an I-told-you-so moment. "We need to get him on *The $64,000 Question.*"

"Is that right?" Graf asked.

"You should see the magazines and books he reads," Anna went on. "Real highbrow stuff. Royce is an intellectual." She said that word like it rhymed with her other favorite: fairy. "Last night he called a stupid painting kitsch. I bet he knows what's playing up there on the fiddle. He could complain about it, critique it, and mean it. Say some more French things, old boy."

"Yeah, say our names in French words," Graf said.

"*Va te faire foutre,*" I offered. *Go fuck yourself.* It was best that neither of them caught the meaning of that. I hoped Graf thought it was his name in French. Being uncomfortable made me ask another question. I talk until I'm loopy when I feel nervous. It's a deficiency, but when words are coming out, I don't think or worry. "Have either of you watched *The Ten Commandments*?" I asked.

Anna said no, and Graf said yes, he had.

"Is it as good as the hype?"

"It's too long," Graf said. "I can't sit and watch something that long."

"I heard it was told in real time."

Graf looked at me, thought about being polite by laughing, and then declined. "I'm just not a big fan of pictures," he said. "I got better things to do." That was the end of that. He flagged the waiter and ordered a bottle of Pinot Noir. When the waiter brought the bottle, we ordered food. Since I was eating on someone else's dime, I went last and got something cheap: the eggplant and tomato gratin.

Graf took a drink of wine and set his eyes on me again. "So here it is," he began. "I know Fawn Bailey likes you, and Anna here vouches for you. And you're artsy enough to be [*he did a this or that gesture with his hand*], so you ain't a threat to me. That's just about good enough. But I gotta see you in action once before I turn you loose."

"That's for the best. It's been a while," I admitted.

"It's not only training wheels, friend." He took another drink. "I take a cut. I always get a cut. No matter how good you are or how much they like you, I get a cut."

I nodded. I wasn't interested in playing power games. I just wanted to make a few bucks and leave. I was set on that. I promised myself that.

Despite my acquiescence, Graf stepped on a soapbox. He leaned his weight on the table, and the candle flickered. His face grew animated, the hard lines accentuated by shadows. I didn't like him a bit, I decided, as if I'd ever been on the fence about the matter. He wanted to be hardboiled, and his actions could be, but the act ate him up inside. There was something anxious in his manner, something nervous he always had to conceal.

"I've had a couple try to elbow in and clear out their own space," Graf said. "That doesn't fly here. This is strictly a one-operation town. It isn't Cincy. You ain't gonna shop around and find a better deal."

"I understand that."

"Do you? You wanna know what happened to the last guy who tried to cut me out?"

I tested the wine. I glanced at Anna. She was growing uncomfortable now, too.

"It's a helluva lot more than you can do with that blackjack of yours." He watched me for a reaction.

"Anna told you about that, did she?"

Graf nodded. He leaned back. "She told me. She said you brained Marsh until he pissed himself. Is she right? Marsh is no slouch."

"You don't have to worry about me," I said. "I got lucky with that one. I just want to make a little money. I have nothing else in it. That's honest."

Graf finished the glass of wine and poured another. He stared through me.

The food came, the waiter did a few flourishes, and then we were alone again in a crowd of murmuring voices and violin music. Steam rose from the gratin. The tomatoes were canned tomatoes.

Graf tucked his napkin and started in on a rabbit stew. I've always found it insightful to watch what people eat and how they eat it. A lot can be gleaned from food choices. That moment is a sum of the past, and when you settle on that you can start to deduce.

Between bites, Graf said, "I got a séance set up for tomorrow night. I want the two of you to lead it. It's the right place to introduce the both of you. You'll get clients from it. Good clients."

"Swell idea," Anna said. She looked at the plate of grilled calamari she'd ordered with quiet disgust. She should've asked what calamari meant. She touched a puckered tentacle, and the thing jiggled.

"Who gets cut out to let us in?" I asked. It was impertinent, but, then again, I was prone to that.

"Oh, you're going to meet him tonight. Anny didn't tell you? His name's Millard Hines. He's a real playboy. You know, just before you came down here, I found Millard had a side hustle. Skimming money. Taking clients on without me knowing it. He got some of the old ladies begging to suck him off, and that got him thinking he was a celebrity. The mayor's wife laid him." Incredulous, he glanced at Anna. "Audrey Ward," he told her. "Hines told me she swallows, and she's 66. What I tell you? Spitters are quitters, honey. Queen Victoria don't rule no more. You gotta get with the program." To me, he went on, "You know how it is. I couldn't replace him until now."

"I'd rather not meet him then."

Graf looked at Anna again. "I think Millard wants to kill me. Did I tell you that?" He shook his head and then looked back at me. "You'll meet him, friend. I'll let you get drunk first, but you'll meet him."

"Come on, Rube, lighten up," Anna said.

"He's gotta know," Graf said. He picked out a piece of meat still on the bone and worked on it. The juice trailed down his chin. He resembled Anna with her hardboiled egg. They were cut from the same cloth. "Now," he said, "what's the violin girl playing?" He tore the meat.

"Poulenc," I said. Maybe she was, maybe she wasn't. I wasn't listening anymore, and Graf didn't know any better.

"Ha! He is a smart one. You ever tried out for a quiz show? Hey, I mean it."

CHAPTER TEN

*T*he pinot noir was light as water, so it hadn't done much for me. Some people can get wine drunk, but I'm not one of them. When Graf recognized the sobriety of his companions, he took us to a bar farther up Fourth Avenue called The Wheelwright Saloon. The name suggested a western theme, but there was nothing like that on the inside. It was a kempt, simple joint, quiet and dark. The bar was beautiful rosewood and mother of pearl without any scarring. The bell on the door was louder than the music. The music came from a cathedral radio on a shelf behind the bartender rather than a jukebox. Typical radio fare: big band and crooner stuff.

After four shots of gin, my head buzzed. I ordered a fifth shot, but I nursed this one rather than throwing it back. Millard Hines, as I understood things, was set to meet us here. Conspicuously, we sat on stools and waited for his arrival.

Graf was getting friendlier (he'd swallowed four pills for dessert at the restaurant), while Anna grew cooler. As she brooded nervously over a whiskey highball, he kept slapping my shoulder and cracking jokes. The jokes, of course, were at my expense. He had one of *those* manners when high, constantly ribbing. For a moment, I thought the bartender, a wisp named Tony, would tell Graf he was getting too loud for the place, but that never occurred. Graf got a few warning looks and nothing more. I tolerated him.

Presently, he was on a track he thought uproariously funny. Straight faced and slurring, he asked if I was mad that the chef had sliced up my eggplant.

I lit a cigarette and rested my elbows on the bar. The music flowed over me. A ceiling fan spread cool air and wafted smoke. "How's that?"

"You know." He smiled and nudged me. He peered at Anna. "He knows."

"I'm lost," I said.

"Ass slappers like you eat cock-shaped foods," he said. "Big, tremendous balls on your plate. If it ain't that, you ain't havin' it." He worked on a highball, the same drink he'd ordered for Anna. He could barely contain himself for the punch line. "I figured they'd ruined that eggplant for you. You prefer the original shape." He laughed for a while and then came back. "Well, is it true or ain't it?"

I stared ahead, watching Tony work. He was cleaning the same glass for the fourth time. "Is what true?"

"You can't go from quiz show to dunce, pal. Is it true that you people eat nothing except cucumbers and bananas and the like? Or an eggplant with two tomatoes. Jeez Louise."

Anna rolled her eyes and shrugged at me, but I'd heard worse.

I peered at Graf. "Where'd you hear that? Only a select few people know that, Mr. Graf." The gin had me addressing him formally. "Most of those people are insiders." I winked at Anna.

Graf straightened, and he gave a defensive shrug. His tolerance for ribbing was as low as mine was high. "Remember who's paying for your drinks," he warned. "That still doesn't tell me if it's true or not."

"It's not, you dope," Anna said.

We sat in silence, listening to the radio music after that.

Finally, Millard Hines entered The Wheelwright Saloon.

"There's our boy," Graf said. He stood from the bar, leaving Anna and me behind. He underwent a transformation that I found chilling. Abruptly, he was dead sober and business-like, as if he were talking to a cop. He walked over and greeted Hines.

Anna slid over to Graf's seat so that she was directly beside me. "What do you think?" she asked.

"About Graf or Hines?" I finished the gin.

"Both."

I didn't feel free to speak my mind, so I said, "It is what it is. He is who he is. I need the money."

She patted my knee. "Such a good boy," she said.

Graf brought Hines to us and introduced everyone. Hines had a striking look. He was tall, broad shouldered, and young. He had large, spatulate hands on which he wore two gaudy rings. He had a strong grip, and I imagined it on my hip. He was dark-headed, suave, and had a fine jawline. His hair was greased and, like Bill Haley, fell in a spit curl on his forehead. If he hadn't run afoul of Graf, he could make it on local television with his act. He'd look better in a turban than most of the television swamis I'd seen. Too, he'd make a good elbow ornament for a widow with money. He was too much for Huntington, and he was about to hit a brick wall hard.

"How do you do?" he said with some charm. His voice was a velvet baritone. There was no tremor, but he was high on something other than alcohol. I saw it in his eyes. Pain pills. Did Hines sense anything wrong with the tableau? Arrogance and greed were two things that made men comatose with stupidity. All he needed was a carrot and stick, and he'd move along.

Graf put money on the bar for Tony. "Let's get moving," he said, and he started for the door.

"Nice specimen," Anna whispered.

"It's a damn shame," I said. My hands were sweating.

• • •

With the four of us packed into the Mercury (me and Anna in the back and Hines in the front with Graf), we drove through the city. It was beyond midnight now, and Huntington was a cemetery with lights. Graf told Hines that Anna was his new girl and I was Anna's brother. I don't know if Hines bought it or not, but he didn't argue. He stayed contained, not moving or talking much. Outwardly, he was neutral, but he'd been in the backseat of a similar situation previously. He had to have been. He would've received a similar lesson to what Graf was trying to convey to me now. *This is what happens when ....* It's hard to feel sorry for a man so stupid, though. If I were Hines, I'd have been a few states clear of Graf by now. The only way I would've been riding into the dark with him would've been with me locked in his trunk.

We headed straight into the darkness at the edge of town. After crossing a steel bridge into Ohio, the streetlights disappeared. The interior of the car was inky. Just voices and Hines' strong cologne.

"Where we heading?" Hines asked. Now he was getting it. It took a crimson-masked executioner appearing on the hood, but he was getting it. He had a nice voice, I noticed. Very. In the darkness it became a radio voice. Once again, I sympathized with the old ladies. He'd be a real draw. Given the opportunity, I'd swallow his children, too.

Graf fed him bullshit. "I told you," he said. "Didn't I? We're meeting a new client. She's real esoteric. Strictly nocturnal."

"How'd she escape us until now?" It was a sensible question, one he should've asked an hour ago.

Graf spewed more shit. "She's got her own network. A cabal from up north. She prefers red-blooded Egyptians to read her tarot, but I got her interested in you. It took some doing, but we got her, I think. You just need to sell it tonight."

I crossed my arms and was cold. A few crummy houses with tiny yards passed by in a blur.

Anna tried her damnedest not to giggle. Maybe she knew Hines better than I did, because I felt sorry for him. This wasn't funny at all. She buried her face against my shoulder, and her back trilled silently. From up front, it looked like we were sharing a joke.

Far from it, I thought.

The car turned onto a back road and started up an incline. The forest closed in. The road was a thin vein through the woods, so narrow that branches scraped the windows. Graf had to wince with each touch. The road snaked upward with the consistency of a stream. Enough of that weaving could make you nauseous. We climbed higher, until the engine warbled from the labor. Finally, the road leveled off and turned to gravel. We rolled until the gravel turned to dirt. The Mercury came to a stop in a clearing framed by old trees, very tall trees without leaves. Up this high, the trees swayed in the wind. The moon was out and, unlike in Cincinnati, thousands of stars were visible in the sky.

Another car, a dark Plymouth from the forties, idled with its headlights glowing. The scene illuminated was not the home of an eccentric client. That was no surprise to anyone in the car, I assumed. I hoped not. Rather, light fell over an informal dumping ground with rusted appliances, gutted furniture, tires, and mounds of trash. Stray cats crawled over the garbage. This was a place where kids got high and broke stuff and where, well, what was about to happen happened.

For the first time, when Hines spoke, a tremor entered his voice. "Listen to me, Mr. Graf. I—"

"—What's gotten into you?" Graf asked. "That's the old lady over there. That's her chauffeur getting out now."

"The hell it is," Hines said. "Just listen to me for a minute. Can I tell my side of things? Can I at least tell what I intended?"

Graf shook his head in the negative. He touched the hard line of a gun in the pocket of his coat. I hadn't been aware he was carrying a piece, but I wasn't surprised. "Get out of the car," he ordered.

Hines gripped the dashboard. With the lights from the Plymouth being the only light inside the car, he was just a shadow fringed with white. "I'm not going anywhere. You're going to turn this car around, and you're going to listen to me." It was hard to watch. My gut wrenched. Anna and I sat like silent judges in the back seat.

"Now you're gonna embarrass me in front of my girl?" Graf said.

"I don't mean it like that. I just—"

"—Get out of the damn car."

"No. I won't do it."

Graf shut off the engine and killed the lights. The beams of the Plymouth still spread across the expanse.

Hines continued to plead his case, getting specific with names and dates and dollar amounts, but Graf had finished talking. He kept shaking his head. That was his sole response.

Across the dump, the door on the Plymouth opened, and a man with the build of a gorilla stepped out. He had the high and tight haircut ordained by the Army. The man strolled over, rolling his shoulders, loosening his knuckles.

Graf extracted his gun. It was no mouse gun like the one Anna possessed. He held a hefty .38, and the long barrel glinted. He looked at us in the backseat. "You two better pile out," he said. "That's Newt. I'll introduce you later." He opened his door and leaned his chair forward, never taking his eyes off Hines. We did as we were told and slid out of the car, leaving behind Hines' cloud of cologne.

"Oh for fuck's sake," Hines was saying. "How was it enough for this?"

"It was more than enough," Graf said.

We stepped back from the car, and I felt exposed. A thought of running toward the road came to mind, but I let it pass. The wind was brutal, rocking the trees and shuddering the blanket of wet leaves on the ground. The gusts were so loud that we didn't hear Hines finish his pleading. We didn't have to hear because the pleading didn't go anywhere or amount to anything. Graf was steadfast. With me as his audience, he had a point to make. Newt came to the door and ripped it open despite Hines' effort to hold the handle from the inside. With a great thrust, the door flung wide and Hines nearly came with it. He hung halfway out of the Mercury. He made an appeal to Newt, about how long they'd known one another, about how they were friends, but Newt looked at him like an insect.

Graf jumped out of the driver's seat and ran around the front of the car. "Drag him out," he ordered.

That was an unnecessary command. The bull already had his hands on Hines' spiffy jacket. He dragged him from the car with ease, pulling him over the leaves and dirt.

Anna saw I was getting queasy. "He deserves it," she assured me. "He might seem like a playboy to you, but he deserves all he's going to get." She, at least, was convinced.

My voice was thin. "I'll take your word for it," I muttered. I had no desire to step in and alter the situation. That's hard for some people to take, but that's how it was. I don't crusade. I felt sorry for Hines, but I didn't know him. I didn't feel anything genuine for him. That didn't mean I wanted to watch, though, and that didn't mean I enjoyed a second of it.

She took my wrist and led me to the front of the car for a better view. I shook with the mix of adrenaline and cold. I looked up at the bright stars and moon, a preferable sight.

Caged, Hines fought back. He kicked, swung, and screamed, but he never got off the ground. His screams did nothing except frighten the strays into hiding. Anytime he managed to get to a knee, Newt battered him, and he went down hard.

Graf played with his gun, aiming it all over the place, gesticulating with the .38. He was getting his rocks off, shouting a litany of grievances at Hines, letting him know that he knew about all the times Hines wronged him. It was, admittedly, a long list. Graf was hoarse when he finished.

"Just give it to him," he said finally. "I'm done." He was out of breath.

Newt, who'd yet to speak a word, grabbed Hines' arms and pinned them to the ground. He put his knee on Hines' gut, cocked his arm, and brought his fist down like a jackhammer. He put all 300 pounds into the blow. The ground on the other side of Hines' skull did some of the work, too. The sound was gruesome as goddamn hell. A thin trail of blood, as if ejected from a syringe, flew onto the bull's jacket. A strike like that and Millard Hines wasn't a pretty man anymore. His nose was smashed and his lip split and it looked like his jaw had become unhinged. He cried out, this time like a boy with a broken bone, and the bull hit him again, just as hard and solid as the first.

"That'll take the fight out of him," Graf said, gleeful and manic. His dick was hard as rebar, watching this unfold. Hines was more than a thief. He was a threat to Graf's manhood.

Hines remained conscious, although barely. His eyes were open. He exhaled, and the pool of blood oozed from his throat and fell over his lips. The spit curl on his head, still cemented in place, looked especially pathetic now.

Newt stood and looked down at his quarry. He rubbed his knuckles. Hines pushed on the ground but failed to rise. He covered his face with his hands. When Newt reached into his coat, I thought for certain he'd pull out a gun. He didn't. He pulled out an old tube sock, stuffed with something that made it a club. The heavy sock dangled from his fist, and he rattled it. The cloth caught the light and gleamed at a hundred pinpoints. Shards of broken glass filled the sock. He swung the weapon like a hammer, bringing the business end down against Hines' forehead. Hines screamed out again. The bull bludgeoned his face and body with the crude weapon, using rapid swings.

I tore free of Anna's grip and walked behind the Mercury. I couldn't take it anymore. I walked all the way to the edge of the clearing, where the trees started and the road began its descent. Since the trees were dead, I saw all the way down the hillside. We must've been three hundred feet in the air. I saw the river and the bridge and Huntington with chains of glittering light on the other side. As the blows continued to land, I thought, *you don't owe Hines anything.* I tried to convince myself, but a touch of guilt crept in. I heard his suffering. *This isn't your fight. It's Hines' and Hines' alone. Would he help you if the situation were reversed? People are animals. It doesn't matter how they treat each other.*

About ten minutes passed before Graf joined me. He was sweating profusely and smiling. He brushed aside his blond hair. "He'll live," was the first thing he said. He lit a cigarette and handed it to me. I'd been so dazed I'd forgotten I wanted to smoke. I took it. Graf looked out over the river with me then. We shared a moment. With the moon a long streak on the water, and with the stars prominent, it was a beautiful sight.

"I can see this from my room," Graf bragged. It mattered to him that I knew that. "You should've got a room on the tenth floor."

"It's not bad at night," I admitted.

"Hey." He touched my sleeve. "Hines will live. Newt knows what he's doing. I'll tell you one thing, though."

"What's that?"

"You won't see Millard Hines anymore. He's leaving the business."

I'd taken that for granted.

"Here." Graf handed over some ten dollar bills, five of them. "He owed me that and more."

I looked at the money, hesitated, and then took it.

"That'll get you started, friend." Graf slapped my back. "Take it as a token of good faith," he said. "It ain't a loan. It's a gift."

I folded Hines' money and tucked it away. Behind me, I heard Anna talking to Newt. She giggled as she spoke. I heard Hines groaning in agony, as well, while the two spoke over him. The son of a bitch still wasn't unconscious. I took a long drag.

"I have to say you took it well," Graf said. "You were cold as ice, friend. I don't think you even blinked. Some guys would curl up after seeing a sight like that. I guess you got a stomach for blood."

"I've seen worse," I said. My look was a practiced one. Inside, I was sick and weak. I was white as a ghost, but the night hid that fact just as the darkness hid garbage and sludge in the river, just as it provided refuge for the strays. More than anything, I wanted to be alone. Graf let me be. I finished the cigarette before turning from the river.

CHAPTER ELEVEN

A grey wall of rain rushed nearer, obscuring hills that overlooked the city and pummeling the river. Traffic slowed the taxi, while the storm moved quickly. A portion of the sky was blue and a portion was ash, and the blue side was losing. The last thing I wanted to do was get my new clothes wet, so I looked out the back window and felt anxious and tried not to coach the driver. I'd dropped most of my bundle on those clothes.

Finally, after blasting his horn at a bewildered pedestrian, the taxi pulled to a stop at the curb outside The Prichard. Here came the rain, I heard the roar, and I had sixty feet remaining between me and shelter. I handed the driver some change and slid free of the backseat. The smartass wished me luck and said he'd put his money on me.

"Bad bet," I muttered.

I'd steamroll an old lady if she stood between the hotel and me, but thankfully that wasn't necessary. I ran like a fool to beat the storm. And I beat it, although just barely. As I got beneath the hotel awning, the torrent hit, drumming the canvas above. The rain poured so hard that beads struck the sidewalk and jumped two feet into the air again. The cab driver, satisfied with the entertainment, pulled away.

Relieved and dry, I stepped into the lobby. It was a busier space than it had been the morning prior. There were women at the payphones and lines three deep behind each box. A couple with children and a lot of luggage argued with the desk clerk about a bill. The clinking of glass came from diners having an early lunch in the restaurant. The din of rain came through walls and windows, but that was cozy now rather than threatening. The darkness of the storm fell over the room, and new lights overhead came on. With a shopping bag full of my old clothes, two bottles of gin, and a carton of Chesterfields, I crossed the lobby with purpose.

I had no reason to feel self-conscious anymore. I'd checked myself out in the mirror before leaving a shop called Wright's, and I looked sharp. A new set of clothes can do wonders, mentally and physically, and it'd been a long time since I'd been in new clothes. I felt golden. I wore everything I'd purchased with Hines' money that morning: a charcoal sports coat, a pressed cream shirt, brown slacks, and two-toned wingtip shoes of brown and white. With generous dashes of 4711, the original *eau de cologne*, I even smelled golden.

The pretty clerk, Dominic, who'd checked me in the previous morning stood outside the restaurant hawking newspapers. He had a small stand full of local papers and those of nearby cities that hugged him like a horseshoe. There were a few magazines, too, but none of the art or movie stuff I liked to read. I walked over and asked if he recognized me in my current form. Some days you just have it in you to be bold. This was one of mine.

"Certainly, sir," he said. His face reddened slightly.

I bought copies of the *Cincinnati Enquirer* and *Herald Dispatch*. I put the papers under my arm and searched his eyes. "I told you we cleaned up well, Dom, did I not?"

"You did, sir. Are you enjoying your stay?"

"Come off it. Do I look good or what?"

"Very good, sir."

"And drop the *sir* bit," I said.

He smiled, made sure no one was in earshot, and said, "The boss likes it. He insists on it."

"I'd rather not have any decorum between us. I'd like to get to know you."

He liked that.

"What time do you get off work?"

"A while yet." He gauged my disappointment, then he added, "But I'm due for lunch anytime now."

"Tell the truth, I'm happy you don't work nights. I was afraid of that."

"I never work nights," he said.

"How about you come up to my room for lunch? I got a couple bottles." I moved the shopping bag so that the glass jingled.

Dominic hesitated. He looked at his hands and then kept his eyes on the tiled floor.

"I'm not going to try anything on you," I promised. "I just want to get to know you. I'll have some food sent up, and we can talk a little."

The din of the lobby washed around me: echoes, voices, rolling wheels, shoes against tile. It was one of those good moments in life, the ones you enjoy remembering.

"It's not that," Dominic said. "How'd you know?" He looked up. "I mean—"

I cut him off. That was supposed to be unspoken, but sometimes you have to teach the inexperienced. "You aren't wearing it on your sleeve if that's what worries you. Get out of this asshole town, and you'll get to know, too. You'll get to where you can't miss after a couple years. Even when a man has a wife and kids around him, you'll know. I knew when I first looked at you, when you snarled at us for being scoundrels."

He reddened again. His shyness surprised me. "Give me thirty minutes," he said, checking his watch. "How 'bout I bring up the food? That'll give me an excuse."

"Fine. I'll have a drink waiting on you," I said.

"Oh, there's one more thing. When I was working the desk this morning, an Italian cat came in with a message for you."

"It wasn't Carlo Pedersoli, was it?" Mr. Pedersoli was far too cheap to travel in search of me, yet I had to ask. Then dread snuck in when I realized it could be a cop on the hunt. When you stop and think about things, the whole world smacks into your backside.

Dominic thought about the name. "No, it was Mario something. I had the message sent up to your room. It'll be there."

I thanked Dominic and told him I'd see him in a bit, and then I turned on my heel toward the elevator. All the way up I kept silent, wondering about the Italian and his message. *Today you have luck*, I thought. *Don't forget that. You have luck, and you have goodwill. Don't be miserable until you know.* The kid who'd previously told me about Gene Autry wasn't in the mood to talk either, so we parted ways at the seventh floor without any exchanges, save for me flipping him a dime. He tipped his cap in thanks. I rushed to the room.

The maid had been in. The bed was tight and the bathroom tidied. I put my bag and newspapers on the bed and prowled around in search of the message. A paper waited on the dresser. The note was done on a typewriter rather than handwritten, and it amounted to a letter more than a message. It came from a man named Mario Girotti. I'd never heard the name until now. He was a stranger to me. He was in Huntington, though, and he wanted to see me, and soon.

I won't repeat the niceties and fluff. The substance of the message boiled down to this: *Anna Vogel isn't who you think she is. You're here to take the fall for something big.* Other than the warning, he didn't provide specifics. I went cold inside and read the letter through again. Girotti was a private investigator from Cincinnati. In case I was skeptical, he provided his credentials and spelled out a license number for me to verify. He urged me, in plain language, to realize that I was being warned rather than threatened. He posed no threat to my safety or freedom. His interest wasn't financial, not in the extraction sense, anyhow. He knew about my record, but he wasn't interested in that. This wasn't about anything except Anna and what she'd done in Cincinnati. What that was he wouldn't put in writing, but he'd explain when I met him. I read one of his lines several times: *Mr. Pembrook, she and Mr. Graf are positioning you to take a fall.*

If I let any of this slip to Anna I'd be in danger, he cautioned in postscript. Not from him, he wasn't the kind to threaten, but from Anna and Graf.

I thought about what had happened to Millard Hines then, where he was and what his face looked like.

I folded the letter and placed it inside the dresser's top drawer. A couple thoughts competed for attention. First, the letter felt sincere. Girotti wouldn't be so open if he had his eyes set on me. He needed my help, and he figured inspiring a little curiosity and worry was the way to get it. That was intuition talking. Second, Anna Vogel was too stupid to orchestrate something so elaborate. The mental horsepower wasn't there. She didn't think that many moves ahead. Friction was her primary catalyst. The counterpoint amounted to greed talking, elbowing for its share of the floor. This was new clothes and a nice hotel room and a job that paid real cash talking. I tried to balance the two thoughts, but nothing worthwhile emerged from the competition. It all left me angry and disoriented. I began coming up with questions. What if Girotti was just another boyfriend? What if this was Marsh or somebody hired by Marsh? I could weave a thousand questions from a kernel of dread. It was a talent that kept me awake at night.

Girotti had closed with an offer to meet this evening at a place called Ritter Park. He said it would be in the open air and there'd be a lot of people around. It was just a community park with benches and walking trails and swing sets. It was in an affluent neighborhood, too, so there would be nothing shady about the meeting. He wanted to soften my doubts. I was intrigued, immediately willing, but the time was no good. I had the séance with Graf. I couldn't meet Girotti. He'd think I stood him up or wasn't interested, because he hadn't left a way for me to get back to him with a message of my own.

What did Anna do? I thought then. A profound question. One could drown in that quagmire.

I busied myself for distraction: putting away my old clothes, opening a pack of cigarettes, opening a bottle of gin, fishing my transistor radio from the laundry bag. I hadn't brought along many possessions, but the radio was something I couldn't do without. The small Regency had brought me a lot of comfort over the past couple years. To an extent, I'd become dependent on its presence. At night I went to sleep with it, and in the morning I woke up with it.

I put the gin and radio on the table in the corner of the room opposite my desk and window. I scanned through stations until I found some music. It came down to two choices: Vivaldi or The Five Satins. I went with the top forty station, the least jarring of the two. Voices warbled through a touch of static. I moved around the radio until the reception cleared.

I was halfway through a cigarette, still dwelling on the Girotti matter, when a knock came at my door. I turned down the volume, Frankie Lymon and the Teenagers were on now, and I walked over to answer. Dominic stood behind a metal serving cart. Two plates of food waited beneath linen tea towels. He smiled, and the smile reached his eyes. He checked up and down the hallway, nervous, and then rushed in as I opened the door wider.

I must've been two different people to him, day and night. Whereas I'd been vivacious and playful not thirty minutes prior, now I brooded. I returned the smile, but it didn't have the verve his possessed. The letter had knocked me to the ground.

My look worried him. For a moment he was crestfallen, like I'd played a joke to catch him up and humiliate him, as if that had happened to him before.

I shut the door. "It isn't you, Dom," I said to reassure him. "Just got some bad news is all." I blew a cloud of smoke.

"I can go," Dominic offered. He wanted to go. He had regrets. He was scared of getting caught.

I dismissed that. "I'd like the company," I said.

A beat of silence passed between us. He lifted the tea towels and showed the food: two ceramic pots filled with soup and a platter of crostini. "Hungry?"

I was. I hadn't eaten anything all day. It smelled terrific. "What'd you bring?"

"Leek and potato soup and some bread. What do you think?"

"Not bad," I said. "A man of refinement and taste."

Dominic shrugged. "I took it from the kitchen. Some fool ordered it and didn't want it anymore."

I laughed, crossed my arms, and took another drag. "How romantic."

His face reddened for the third time. "Truth be told I'm a little short on funds," he admitted.

I couldn't say much about that. I was wearing the only funds I had.

He rolled the cart over to my table where the radio played and my previous cigarette roiled in the ashtray. The Chordettes came through the tinny speaker. He served the food, and I poured drinks. He wanted club soda with his gin, so I obliged. We sat in hard wooden chairs, and I left the radio on with the volume low. The soup was warm, and the bread had a nice crunch to it.

Outside, rain beat against the windowpane. Despite the hour, it was dark with storm clouds. I'd switched on the lamp beside the bed on the opposite side of the room. The low light had the effect of candlelight. Looking at Dominic, I felt romantic.

When I placed an unfinished cigarette in the ashtray, Dominic picked it up and put it in his mouth. The shaft of it rested on his lip, and he let it hang like that. The sight went right through me. It stirred me. With his slicked dark hair and eyes a shade of pale emerald, he had me, then and there, smitten. I hadn't seen a beautiful face like his in some time. His skin was smooth and his body long and slender. He had my blood rushing.

He gestured at the radio. "You like that stuff?" he asked.

I crunched another piece of bread. Between bites, I said, "I like everything. Vivaldi was on the other station, and I can listen to him, too, when the mood suits me. Doesn't really matter. The noise is what I like."

"Who's Valveteen?" he asked. "Or Valvoline. Or whatever you said."

You can't have everything, I suppose. Such is the lottery of birth. I let it go. "Doesn't matter," I said. "What do you like?"

"I'm more of a Gene Vincent and Elvis Presley guy. Harder stuff. I like some drive behind it."

"I'm up for anything," I said.

He finished the cigarette and started on the soup again. Either it wasn't to his liking or he was too embarrassed to eat in front of me. He tore a piece of bread into shreds, deciding. "I play in a group, you know? We play around town some weekends. I play guitar. I'd like for us to get something recorded one day. King Records is in Cincinnati. That ain't too far."

"Just two hours," I said. At least, I thought, he was the creative type. I admired that.

"Bill Beach plays around Huntington, and he did a record with King. *Peg Pants.* I got the record at home."

I'd never heard of Bill Beach or *Peg Pants.* Honestly, I wasn't schooled on rock and roll. "What's the name of your band?"

Dominic laughed. "We change that every month or so. Right now it's The Coup de Villes. There are a hundred groups called that, though. We'll change it. You should come see us."

"You tell me when, and I'll be there."

He ripped at the bread some more. "You like movies?"

"I love them."

He leaned onto the table. "Oh, me too. What do you go for most?"

"Anything and everything. I used to work at a theater, and I watched everything."

"I'll tell you the type I can't get enough of: UFOs and aliens and all that." He ticked off a few: *It Came from Outer Space, The Thing from Another World, Earth vs. the Flying Saucers, Invasion of the Body Snatchers.* "I see every one of 'em, good or bad."

I smiled at this enthusiasm. Girotti's letter had brought me down, and Dominic was lifting me up again. Not everyone can do that. You have to seek out the people who can, and I had one across the table from me. He wasn't much younger than me, I noticed. Five years. Ten at the most. "I watched *Invasion of the Body Snatchers* three times," I admitted.

"Didn't your boss ever get pissed?"

I nodded. "Sure he did. When he caught me. I was sly about it, though. Most of the time he didn't know any better."

"That's a job I wouldn't mind. You gotta know somebody to get on at the Keith-Albee here. Hey, can I call you Royce?"

"I was hoping you would."

He leaned back and sipped at the gin and soda. "What do you do for a living now, Royce?" he asked then. "This place ain't cheap. Mr. Graf ain't cheap. The woman you came in with certainly ain't cheap."

I laughed about Anna and Graf not being cheap, but he thought I was laughing out of embarrassment for the work I did.

"Hey, I can't say anything. Look at me. I work at a damn hotel."

"Believe it or not, I do séances, read fortunes, things like that."

"You're kidding." His smile grew wider. "Like county fair stuff? Like swamis in turbans?"

I nodded. "Honest. Do you think that's crazy?"

"It's a little wild," he admitted. "I like it, though. Is it real when you do it?"

"Not even slightly real. I make it all up. Everybody makes it up."

"Do you do them here?"

"I have a séance tonight, in fact. But it's a private party."

"Maybe you could read my fortune one day," Dominic said.

"As long as you promise not to believe a word of it, I'll do it."

"You can tell me I'm going to do a record and make it big." He laughed. "You'll have me swooning. Flattery gets you everywhere with me."

"You got it."

He glanced at his watch and frowned. "Break's up," he said. He stood and began to clear the pots and silverware. I'd eaten everything down to the last crumb, but he'd eaten only a couple bites of the soup.

I stood with him. As he organized the cart, I stepped around and gave him a quick kiss on the cheek. He was a couple inches taller than me, so I had to get on my toes to accomplish it. Yet again, he blushed.

"I'd like to do this again, Dom," I said.

He smiled. "Yeah, I would, too. Thanks for the drink." He took a pad from his jacket. "You got a pencil?"

I went over to the dresser and found a pen for him.

He jotted down his address. "Call on me," he said. This time he leaned in to kiss me. It was a peck on the lips. I could've thrown him on the bed then, but I refrained. I wanted things to be genuine. "I hope your bad news wasn't too bad," he added.

"You made things better," I said.

He took the cart and left. I shut the door softly behind him.

Alone again, I poured another drink and sat down beside the radio. Dominic had shone some light on me, but with his absence the shadows gathered. I drank, smoked, and worried about Mario Girotti and Anna. I retrieved Girotti's letter and read through it again just to torture myself. The radio droned, and the rain kept up. I switched off the lamp.

CHAPTER TWELVE

With familiarity, Graf opened a wrought iron gate that held patterns intricate as lace. The three of us walked along a trim stone pathway into the folds of a garden. Anna told me I'd admire the place, and she was correct. The Blum mansion was a Victorian beauty, replete with a geometric turret that rose above the trees. Between the gate and the home stretched the most elaborate and expensive garden in the city. According to Graf, the garden was a patchwork of color and exotic shapes during summer months, with ferns, fruit trees, and tufts of poison to keep destructive vermin distant. For now, being October and cold, the garden approached its skeletal, winter shape. The petals had gone, and the leaves were falling. Color came from leaves that clung to life, from Halloween pumpkins atop an arbor, and from the lurking shapes of tabbies that patrolled the yard. Rain, after a full day of storms, slicked vines that climbed the Blum façade. Light from passing cars caught the fish scale shingles.

I sheltered my cigarette from a chill breeze and worked it down. On one hand I had my nerves, but on the other I was eager. I questioned why I'd waited so long to get back to this life. Simultaneously, I questioned why I hadn't heeded Girotti's warning and met him. I was playing with fire. It's hard to explain, but, approaching the manor, I was important, I felt I was on the preferable side of the gate. Before ascending the ornate landing, I discarded my cigarette into one of the flowerbeds. The home wasn't a place to be soiled with smoke.

Graf rang the doorbell, and we waited. Finally, a woman answered. The heavy oak door, painted red, opened inward. The woman possessed the feline grace of Anna, but she wasn't worn out and ragged. Her manner was one of refinement. She wore a green woolen dress with a silver clasp at the neck. Her dark hair, touched with grey and cut in a bob that reached her cheekbones, was reminiscent of the 1920s.

Anna and I stood at Graf's shoulders. He'd advised us to look "mystical," as if we bore the weight of the dead on our backs, and to keep our eyes on the ground with an air of "contemplative gloom." These were his words. He'd fed us coffee, amphetamines, gossip, and visions before driving out. She and I were buzzing. After Millard Hines' indiscretions, Graf didn't want his mediums to appear as anything save for humble, so eyes must remain down. To an obnoxious degree, Graf knew exactly how he wanted things: two servants at the beck and call of a great man. He played the great man, one who'd looked beyond the veil to the afterlife and survived a vicious blow to the mind. I don't see how anyone got that vibe from Graf, but that's the product he sold. Unless human nature changed a hundred miles upriver, then it was the type of theatrics for which people in a mansion like this would pay heartily.

Naturally, the great man took the lead now. "Good evening, Professor Cole," said Graf.

The woman looked at Anna and me. Although no change came over her countenance, her displeasure was palpable. The lack of enthusiasm, the stony glare, told us everything.

"Where's Millard?" she asked. "We were expecting Mr. Hines."

Graf navigated the situation carefully. "I have discussed the matter with Mr. and Mrs. Blum," he began. "Unfortunately, and this is as painful to me as it must be to you, Professor Cole, Millard Hines has decided to leave the city. I begged him to stay, positively begged him because he means a great deal to me and all of us, but he insisted on going south to Savannah."

Bruised, the professor asked, "Without saying goodbye?" She was leaving us to stand out in the cold, belying her grace and manner, but she didn't notice or care. "He always spoke of Savannah," she said faintly. It was apparent that she had more than séances going on with Hines. Professor Cole, I assumed, was one of the reasons Hines had fallen from grace.

"It appears so," Graf said. "Millard is a driven man."

"A force of nature," Professor Cole agreed. "He must follow his visions." She took a breath and tried to recover, but the news had left her shaken.

"This has all been explained to Mrs. Blum," Graf continued. "I would like to introduce you to new talent tonight. Mrs. Blum has agreed. You have *my* assurance of their quality. This is Anna Vogel, and this is Royce Pembrook. I have called them in from Philadelphia, all at my expense, to complete our work here. Miss Vogel and Mr. Pembrook, this is Adeline Cole. She is a professor of literature at the college and a *great* student of the occult. A very brilliant woman, she is. No doubt you can sense her luster."

Lust, perhaps, is more apropos, I thought.

As directed, we nodded with humility but said nothing.

Adeline Cole opened the door further and beckoned everyone inside. Now she was curious. The turn was slight, but it was a step toward us rather than away. The warmth of the house went through my body like I'd opened an oven. Professor Cole, standing eye to eye with me in the heels she wore, displayed an uncertain frown. I met her gaze solemnly, but still I said nothing. I gave her the thousand-yard stare, and chill bumps rose on her slender arms.

These people. All it takes is a look. When Graf said, "look mystical," he knew what he was talking about, absurd as it was.

"It's horrible, isn't it, for a man to leave so suddenly?" Adeline asked. Over her shoulder, in the main parlor, a tangle of voices emerged. The crowd was early and eager.

"It's that and more," Graf agreed.

She closed out the night, snuffing the wind with a hiss. "I'm the coat lady for the evening," she said. She took the coats worn by Graf and Anna, but I didn't have anything except the sports jacket. I preferred to keep it on. My hands were red blocks of ice.

A man with a jovial peasant face came into the front hall then. Briskly, he passed a wall of 19th century portraits, some sepia, some faded grey. He was a short man, somber, built with the strength of an ox, and with hands harder than most in his life station. He'd been rich for a long time, but I couldn't tell whether he'd been born that way or not. I doubted it.

"Mr. Blum," Graf said.

Arthur Blum had made his money in railroad speculation, I was told, and now he served as president of Marshall College. His real passion, his obsession, was Spiritualism. For the past three decades, Blum had devoted his life to the Spiritualism of Arthur Conan Doyle and Oliver Lodge. Men of his generation, the Lost Generation as they were called, were part of the original ghost craze in the 1920s. Had Blum lived in an earlier age, I was told, he would've been labeled a zealot. His obsession was that absorbing. He even possessed a letter from the Sherlock Holmes' author, which was framed on his parlor wall above the table where séances were conducted. His wife, Genevieve, was a "sensitive," he claimed, but she was too fragile to practice the art of divination. He liked to think of himself as sensitive to the afterlife, as well, a man of keen nose, yet just by looking at him I saw that a combination of obsession and grief drove him.

"Mr. Graf," Blum said. "I was heartily sorry to learn that Mr. Hines departed our circle. My wife was very fond of him. The news brought her to tears. She's scarcely recovered from it."

"It's truly a shame," Graf said. "I wished him well. As Professor Cole so adroitly put it, he is 'a force of nature.' I urged him to come speak with you before leaving, but the pull was too great, too urgent. He simply refused to be derailed."

Blum's feelings about Hines were more complicated than those of Adeline Cole or Mrs. Blum, I sensed, but he let the matter slide. Despite his words, I didn't get the sense that Hines' absence displeased him. His speech felt rehearsed.

"May I introduce our mediums for tonight?" Graf asked.

Blum looked us over. His gaze lingered on me. "I sense something about this man already," he said.

I looked up from the ground, looked him in the eye.

Blum nodded. "Bring them in here. I'd like to get my wife's impression simultaneously with my own."

My hands got to sweating. Blum sensed my acting talent, I feared. A mix of anticipation and feeling like an imposter came down on me. The latter wasn't terminal, but it was present. It put me on edge. The amphetamines didn't do anything to slow my heart.

Arthur Blum led us into a candlelit parlor. A cloying

mustiness, perfumed, floral, with a hint of tobacco, filled the air. The tableau was charming and properly mysterious, what one would expect from a man who'd lived in the age of Houdini. Eclectic possessions, time capsules from three decades prior, crowded the windowless room: a phonograph with a horn, expressionistic paintings of the German school, and a table crafted from yew, too nicked and battered for this stately home, but endowed with an ethereal buzz in its fibers. Spiritualists prefer instruments ripened by vibrations, like fine violins. Mica inlay trimmed the table's edges.

In this business, Spiritualists were the easiest people with which to deal. No truer cliché than "preaching to the choir" applied. Not only did the average Spiritualist lack skepticism, they were desperate to believe. Believing was a badge of "open-mindedness." Spiritualists were predictable, too, right down to the mise en scène.

Before introducing anyone at the table, Blum showed us letters from Sir Arthur Conan Doyle and the other Spiritualist pontiff, Sir Oliver Lodge. Doyle and Lodge had written the gospels of Blum's faith, books full of rambling dementia like *Raymond, Or Life and Death*. Literature and paraphernalia of a more recent practitioner, Edgar Cayce, occupied another corner of the room. Blum gave a cursory tour of this portion of his collection, as well. Everyone waited politely as he did so. *Humor the patriarch* was a maxim by which the group lived.

Photographs of at least one of the trio, Doyle, Lodge, or Cayce, were framed in every room of the mansion, and there were a lot of rooms. Blum showed us the letters and artifacts like they were accreditation, and it fascinated me that he asked for nothing like that in return from us. Graf's word satisfied him. That was why Graf got the money. He'd done the groundwork and cultivated trust. I could only imagine what bullshit

Graf fed Blum about our pedigrees, our mystical learning in Shangri-La and Atlantis.

Blum then introduced Anna and me to his wife, Genevieve. With blonde hair barely covering her ears and curled under at the bangs, she was graceful and elegant and stylish. She wore large rings on her fingers and dressed in a satin robe, flowing like water over her arms, and ending at the neck, wrists, and ankles in fur trim. Unlike Anna's imitation, Genevieve wore real mink. There was one thing, however, I found to be inelegant about the woman: her grey eyes were like dead orbs. She'd suffered a lot of trauma, I concluded. Her eyes were closed even when open. I tucked that away. She'd be an easy nut to crack.

Blum then introduced us to his guests. There were, on either side of Genevieve Blum, Spiritualists from the college and community: a physicist named Helms, a political scientist named Weaver, Audrey Cole Ward, Adeline's matronly sister and wife to Huntington's mayor, Professor Hawkins, an elderly historian, Professor Hawkins' wife Dina, wearing horn-rimmed glasses, and, lastly, a psychologist named North. North was the newest member of the circle, or "the church family" as Blum called his group.

Graf took a seat beside Adeline Cole. Despite Adeline being ten years her senior, I don't think Anna liked that much. Regardless, Anna behaved. She and I filled the two chairs at the head of the table. Eyes fell on us. Blum extinguished all the candles except for one. For a moment, we let the darkness and mood settle. Then Anna said a few things about joining hands and feeling vibrations in the room, in the house, the city, the state, the whole universe. We traveled outward, one concentric sphere at a time.

I'd planned an outline of the séance with Anna and Graf. It

was a loose construction, and we'd go on instinct as needed. Improvisation was our art, after all. Graf gave us plenty of ammunition to reel in the Blums and their guests. I was aware of all the traumas of everyone seated at the table.

I surveyed the congregation. I'd yet to say a single word.

"Mark the date, Mr. Blum," Anna said. "October the 9th." She drew a shaky breath. I squeezed her hand.

Blum had a leather bound notepad in front of him. He wrote down the date with an expensive pen. He'd be writing down everything. The man was breathless with anticipation. No chicanery would be too much for him, so Anna and I gave them a show. Before entering trances, we unclasped hands to break the ring, then joined again to renew the ring, and then Anna asked for questions from the customers. For the most part, they wanted to know the usual stuff. The grief component was never far from these ceremonies.

The Blums asked for contact to be made with their son, whom they had lost in 1926. He was their only child. Upon this we advanced first.

"Madam Vogel, begin," I said.

Anna reclined her head against the back of her chair. Her throat pulsed, and her jawline stood out prominently. In a soft, practiced voice, chanting more than singing, she recited a verse from an old ballad called *Pretty Polly*. It was, Anna claimed in her act, irresistible bait for a spirit guide she used named Spider John. It was agreed that we would use her gimmicks rather than mine.

> *Oh where is Pretty Polly, quite near she stands*
> *With rings on her fingers and lily-white hands*
> *We walked a pace farther and what did we spy?*
> *A newly dug grave and a spade lying by*

Her voice trailed off, letting the lyrical bait linger. It was cheese to the mouse, she claimed. Air in the parlor took on new weight. The ludicrous song was a favorite of Spider John. As Anna often relayed to her clientele, this John had died in 1881, gutted by a group of Comanche while prospecting for silver in Arizona. She'd come up with the character while watching *The Treasure of the Sierra Madre*, I believe. I imagined him as Walter Huston.

Tonight I was Spider John. His reedy voice came from my throat. My impression of Walter Huston was befitting *Looney Tunes* and unfit for business, so I went with another voice. I made Spider John sound like something from *Inner Sanctum Mystery*, and I pretended he had the mercurial consistency of weather: playful, morose, angry, solemn, and cruel in turns.

One leg of the table lifted and fell with a bang. That was Graf's contribution. A shudder passed through the crowd.

Spider John was just warming up. "Arthur," I said. "Charlie is speaking to me. He is here. He sits on the bank of a river, watching the water."

"He always did," Arthur said. "He loved the water."

"The water is helping him adjust. He doesn't move when the river grows tumid and reaches his feet. He lets it swell around him. Charlie is adjusting. He's finding his voice. It takes many years for some, Arthur, but this child has tremendous strength. It can take millennia to adjust properly. He's only been here thirty years." Graf had told me everything, and he had the audacity to tell the Blums he'd told me nothing.

"Dear Christ," Arthur choked. "What does he say, John?" He wrote as he spoke, scrawling frantically to keep pace.

"John, does Charlie hurt?" Genevieve asked.

The audience waited in silence as I grimaced and formed answers. The Blums found the water angle touching, so, with philosophical gravity, I provided more analogies. "He feels no physical pain," I said then. "I'm very close to him now. It isn't easy to steal his attention from the river."

Arthur laughed, pleased with a memory.

"His wounds are healed," I said. "The only pain Charlie feels is that he misses you dearly. He would like to talk to you more. He sees you, often, on the surface of the water, when the waves are calm. He sees you, and he remembers. He's grinning now. He's remembering right now, Arthur."

Arthur looked up from his pad. "What is it? What is he remembering?"

"Arthur, you took his hand and led him along a dock. He is very young. You led him onto a steamboat. An old steamboat from Mark Twain days. The two of you, just the two of you, traveled the river. You traveled the Ohio and the Mississippi all the way to New Orleans. There were others on board, but to Charlie it was just the two of you."

"I remember him saying that to me," Arthur breathed. He leaned back in his chair, faint. "I remember." Shaken, he'd stopped writing. Genevieve took the pad from him and jotted down what remained.

"You're remembering simultaneously," I said. "Do you feel the connection? Charlie does. He's grinning, Arthur."

Blum's mouth was slightly agape. He nodded. "I feel it," he said.

The line about Arthur and Charlie being the only two on board was a lucky hit. Graf hadn't fed that information. If chess, the gambit would decide the winner.

"What else does he remember?" Arthur asked, wanting to remember more alongside his son. The feeling, if one believed it, was intoxicating.

I rummaged for material to shape, taking time. The parlor was silent save for breathing. The water was too poignant a theme to relinquish, so I said, "He's telling me about an earlier time now. It's the teens and the three of you are having a night at the cinema."

"*20,000 Leagues*," Genevieve said. "It was 1916."

"To him it's a great work of art playing on the screen." I laughed, and in the moment it was Charlie laughing through Spider John. "It's *20,000 Leagues Under the Sea*, and my mother, Mrs. Blum rather—"

"—No," Genevieve interjected. "Say it that way, please."

"My mother," I continued, "is talking about the *Nautilus* and Captain Nemo, and father is laughing because he can't tell whether mother or I like the picture best. He tells us so. And mother, she continues to tell me things. The picture made her think of Atlantis, and she tells me about Atlantis and Plato and the Pillars of Hercules." I slowed, stopped, and caught my breath. "Atlantis," I said, and I smiled.

I caught Graf's eyes. He, too, was smiling.

"He always loved the idea of Atlantis," Genevieve said. To Arthur, she remarked, "Mr. Hines never caught such an idea as that. Never."

Arthur shook his head. "Is it the water that makes Charlie remember these things?" he asked. "Is that why he stays by the river?"

I built on the question, talking more in the abstract to get away from concrete events. Together, we explored Charlie's mindset. I tried to exercise caution when my thoughts grew too fantastic. With their comments, the Blums gave me more material. I talked of the myriad cats Genevieve owned when Charlie was a child. At one point, the cats walked along the riverbank and joined Charlie. I tried not to describe them too closely.

Our next target was Audrey Cole Ward. After that, it was

Adeline. The questions came all night, flowing, providing a steady stream of material. I didn't have to generate much of anything. I only shaped what was given. We improvised on the themes like jazz musicians while the customers did most of the work. To ensure that the "church family" would be hungry for more, we did not cover everyone at the table. Some questions were left unanswered.

We were, in the end, a hit.

CHAPTER THIRTEEN

It was after 11pm when Graf pulled to the curb outside The Wheelwright Saloon. Being a Tuesday night, the crowd on Fourth Avenue was thin. He shut off the Mercury and looked around at me in the backseat. He wore a goofy smile I didn't like. Anna was busy laughing, so much so that she was doubled over with tears in her eyes. She'd taken a few colorful pills after leaving the séance, and she was high as rent. The two of them had been needling me about Arthur Blum the entire drive.

I'd made a splash with the man, apparently. He'd taken a fancy to me after sensing my "power," he'd confided in Graf. Blum had taken me aside and confessed much the same thing. He said he sensed my soul was "immeasurably" old, that I'd lived through generations going all the way back to Atlantis. What do you say to that? In my current environment, it behooved me to agree with him, so I did. I said I'd tell him about my time in Egypt as Imhotep one day. He invited me to dinner at his home so he could pick my brain. Genevieve told him I'd been part of the French Revolution. She said I'd been caught between the hammer and anvil by the Terror, and that I'd been guillotined. She sensed this quite strongly. Graf and

Anna loved that piece of information. If Girotti was honest, I understood why they thought that hilarious.

"There are worse things than sugar daddies," Graf told me. He wiped his eyes. "Just remember what we talked about yesterday, friend." He meant Hines, of course. In other words: *Don't let the flattery go to your head. You're a man in my employ. Don't hatch any get rich schemes. Remember who got you in the door, and remember Newt.* No menace touched his voice. It could've been a remark about litter on the sidewalk. It was what it was. You do this and I'll do that. He didn't respect me anymore than a cockroach.

Anna's head was bobbing now like she was about to crash. She was peaks and valleys with nothing between. I reached up and shook her. It wouldn't do us any good for her to smash her nose against the dashboard.

"You feeling okay?" I asked. She'd eaten a lot of pills. A fistful. Now she was about to chase the cocktail with hard liquor. I hadn't been around her enough to know how much she could take. She was a veteran of it, though. That much was certain.

She turned around and looked at me. Perhaps she was inside a dream for a moment, because she got candid and asked through the dark, "What'd he tell you?" She didn't mean Arthur Blum.

Guardedly, I asked, "What'd who tell me?"

Graf stayed busy wiping his eyes. He was higher than Anna. He rubbed until his eyes were bloodshot, like his loose eyelash was an insect, and he couldn't stand the touch of it.

Anna smiled the way lushes smile, like they have something on you. "You know, old boy," she slurred. "He told you about me, didn't he? What'd he tell you?"

Mario Girotti, I thought. She knew about the private

investigator. I didn't know what to do with that information, so I played dumb. Ignorance was the best defense I had.

I let her unfocused stare trail off, and we got out of the car. Anna was grooved, though, and wouldn't let go of the matter. She hugged me, pressing me off the curb and against the Mercury, and Graf didn't care. Her breath was hard and warm against my face. It smelled rancid, like she had a rotten molar. "He won't tell you anymore," she said. She kissed me on the cheek. "Not another word. You missed that boat. Be open with your friends next time."

Graf walked over, his eye red as a blister. "Watch it, fairy, that's my girl," he quipped.

I disentangled myself and straightened my jacket.

Graf laughed at his joke so loud that the noise ricocheted down the Fourth Avenue corridor. That was one way, perhaps the best way, to get the cops on us. I wanted away, and fast. Anna stared at me.

When the joke settled, Graf asked, "You comin' inside or what, fancy?"

I declined the invitation. "I think I'll walk back," I said. It was only four or five blocks to The Prichard. I needed free of Anna.

Graf shrugged and then put his arm around Anna. "He could suck Blum's old cock tonight and get a room for free," he said. The joke didn't penetrate Anna's fogged brain. She was so gone now that Graf propped her up. His knuckles whitened with the effort. She'd hit the pavement if he didn't provide a crutch. Neon light fell over the couple.

I didn't like her odds against the liquor, but I told her to drink her heart out. I wished she would.

Graf told me to "dream big dreams" and something smart ass about Atlantis, and then he headed inside the bar.

I lit a cigarette. Being alone, even for that second, was a weight lifted. I started walking, and that slowed the buzz in my head. There weren't many people out, and those who were paid little attention to me. I passed by unseen. I remained jarred by the evening, the séance, the speed, Mario Girotti (pieces of all these things got whisked around in my mind), but the crisp, cold air had a soothing effect. I finished one Chesterfield and lit another. Then another after that. I had decisions to make. I couldn't shuck the responsibility much longer. If I put it off, I'd end up caged.

I walked in the direction of the Greyhound station, which was the opposite of The Prichard. At first, I had no destination in mind. I just kept walking to the next street light. Eventually, I passed the art deco terminal and thought, *I have money for a ticket now*. That was a prime option. *Could I convince Dominic to leave with me?* I thought. I didn't know enough about him to know what anchored him here, if anything. Then I thought about the address he had given me. Dominic lived in the 900 block of 16th Street. The thought, the potential of a visit, got my heart racing.

The distance wasn't a bother. I needed the air. I made a right, crossing traffic and starting up 16th Street. Marshall College, where Arthur Blum served as president, stood across the road at my left. Fourth Avenue ended at the front edge of the campus. A large brick building rose behind a stand of trees. Seeing the campus dredged up a memory: when I was a child, I was slated to attend Brown University, where my mother, Eva, went to school (at the university's Pembroke College for women), but that didn't materialize after my grandfather went bust. The money simply wasn't there, and I'd been a terrible student in grade school. My life would've been very different if I'd gone to Brown. Looking at the dark trees and stone walkways, a surge of resentment came over me. Although I often blamed my grandfather for changing the course of my life, my mother was the one who brought scandal into our family. She was to blame for my grandfather's troubles. She was the beginning of his troubles. Everything else followed.

Beyond Sixth Avenue the streets were deserted and quiet, and the lights were sparse. I crossed under a jet dark viaduct and emerged on the other side of the railroad tracks. I carried the blackjack in my pocket but nothing else. My footfalls on the damp sidewalk, a noise that brought my vulnerability into focus, had me wishing I carried a pistol. Then again, Huntington wasn't Cincinnati. Street gangs weren't a problem here. No hoodlums jumped out or blocked my path. The poor sections of town were just poor.

For the thousandth time that day, I thought about Girotti. I knew nothing about the detective, and yet I had a picture in my mind of an overweight, unshaven man in a cheap suit. He was a man who skulked around and followed people and lived in a seedy building where he worked out chess problems because he wanted to be Philip Marlowe. The image was straight from pulp magazines.

How different would things be right now if I'd met with him? Would I have ever got into a car with Anna and Graf? And how the hell did Anna know about the private detective? Was he that sloppy? Or did somebody in the lobby tip her off?

The questions were frustrating, and I couldn't answer any of them.

I was surprised when 16th Street led me to a block of project housing. Here there rose plain brick buildings, artless two-story squares with thin windows, metal doors, and concrete slabs for porches. The buildings resembled military bunkers. As a unit, they encased the entire block. A single streetlight buzzed on and off. A pack of dogs rummaged around a dumpster. Two Black youths, leaning on a wire fence and smoking something that wasn't a cigarette, watched as I entered their neighborhood. I kept my eyes on the cracked sidewalk. Thankfully, the kids didn't call after me. They didn't follow. They simply watched me like the stray dogs watched me.

Finally, I arrived at the address Dominic had given me. He lived in room number three of the outermost building. I understood what it was like to stay in a hellhole like this. I stepped up to the concrete pad and considered going through the front door. It stood ajar, warped steel incapable of fully closing, let alone locking. A sawed-off chain hung from the handle. I looked up at the windows. There were no lights in any of them. I wondered if Dominic was sleeping or if he'd gone out tonight. It was ludicrous, considering the few times I'd been around him, but a tinge of jealousy went through me while considering the latter. I didn't know him. I had to check myself and remind myself of that fact. Like a creep, I was standing on his front stoop in the middle of the night. He didn't know me. I cared about him because he looked good and I *wanted* to care about him. It was superficial. It was nothing.

It had been a long time for me. That was the real reason. It'd been years since I'd had a relationship that amounted to anything more than throwaway sex. Getting fucked wasn't the problem. There were a handful of bars in Cincinnati where I could get what I wanted whenever I needed it. I knew the language to get inside and avoid cops at those places. That was enough to keep me going, but it never amounted to companionship. My last true relationship had been with Charles in 1944. Twelve goddamn years had passed since then. Funnily enough, I'd had an image of Charles in my head when speaking for Charlie Blum earlier that night.

Unlike Charlie Blum, who'd died in an automobile accident, my Charles had been drafted into the army. He'd shipped to the Pacific via San Francisco, and, as far as I knew, he was dead now. After six letters, I'd never heard from Charles again. I didn't know one way or the other, if he was alive or dead. A lot of people died on those islands, so, if he had been killed, he wasn't unique. And he wasn't unique if his body was too mangled to identify or if his corpse never returned in a casket. That happened every day in 1944. I had no contact with Charles' family. I'd never met his parents, and they never knew about me. I thought about writing them a few times, but I never worked up the courage to do so. I had a recurring dream where I'd see Charles on the street somewhere, and I'd go up to him, and he wouldn't know me anymore. He'd returned unharmed, but he didn't care about me. It was still a hole without closure, even after twelve years. Dominic reminded me of Charles in the best ways. He stirred inside me what Charles had once stirred.

Bleary eyed, I decided against heading into the dark beyond the door, and I got back on the sidewalk. Too many memories made my head a mess. *I'll see you in the morning, Dom,* I thought, looking up at the windows without shutters. Single pane, cheap glass. Project rooms got bitterly cold. I started the last cigarette in my pack and walked on.

Someone, a kid I presumed, had left a jack-o'-lantern in the middle of the brick street, hoping either a car would smash it or flip trying to avoid it. I stepped over and picked up the pumpkin. The stub of a dead candle lay inside. The face was more comical than grotesque. It was an early Halloween prank. I've always liked Halloween. I'm not usually a thief, not in the traditional sense, but I carried the jack-o'-lantern away. I don't know why. With it tucked under my arm, maybe I wanted to feel like Brom Bones scaring Ichabod Crane. Maybe I wanted to keep it. Maybe I was just tired and delirious. Eventually, I smashed the jack-o'-lantern against a pile of cinder blocks. The thing smelled rotten, so I didn't want it anymore. Nobody sniped at me for the destruction.

CHAPTER FOURTEEN

Before returning to The Prichard, I stopped at an all-night gas station. The place was deserted save for a car with tailfins in the lot and a single attendant in his shack. An awning with sodium lights covered two pumps. The station was like a beacon at the edge of the dark street. I stepped up to the shack, rubbing the cold out of my hands, and the clerk slid back his window. He picked up a metal coffee can and spat a gob of tobacco juice in it. It was a nice sound.

"Evenin," he drawled. He wiped his mouth with his sleeve. A Confederate flag patch, sewn onto his blue shirt above his name, suited his accent. His name was Ernie. He looked around for my car, puzzled. "Where'd you come from?" he asked. He looked at the empty pumps.

"Out for a walk," I said.

He stared at me. "Cold for a walk, ain't it?"

I pointed at his flag. "You know the difference between Commies and Confederates?" I asked.

He stared at me some more.

"The Commies have won a war."

"Huh?"

I couldn't help myself. "Okay, I can do better. You know what the real flag of the Confederacy looks like?"

"What?"

"Solid white, just like its fan base."

He furrowed his brow. "What'd you say about Commies?"

I bought a couple packs of Chesterfields and, for a quarter, an out-of-date issue of *Screenland* with Debbie Reynolds and a story about Audie Murphy on the cover. The tobacco-chewing clerk smelled like beer. He gave me too much change. I didn't know him well enough to feel bad, so I pocketed the money.

As I turned to go, he asked, "Were you callin' me a Red? I need to know. 'Cause, if you did, I need to come out there and whoop your ass."

"No, not at all. I'm calling you the opposite. You guys lost."

He muttered some more and then slammed his window shut. I was fortunate he didn't chase me down.

I got back on the sidewalk and started toward the hotel again. I lit a cigarette. Just as I got free of the gas station lights, a car approached from behind and painted everything white. I looked over my shoulder, blinding myself, expecting the car to speed by and leave me in darkness. To my disappointment, the car slowed, and the beams stayed on me like spotlights. I assumed it was the police looking to harass someone, looking for some fun. An image of Jimmy the Cop having me alone out here didn't please me. The car slowed beside me, and I kept walking. The hair on my neck stood. I worked on the cigarette with rapid intakes. I halted, though, when I realized the car wasn't a black and white. Rather, the vehicle was an expensive and conspicuous road hog: a dark Chrysler Imperial. The grill and fender glistened, even at this hour. A streak of chrome ran down the side.

The car rolled to a stop. The passenger window came down.

From the dark interior, scarcely louder than the engine, came the voice of Arthur Blum. "Mr. Pembrook," he was saying.

With the magazine hanging from my grip, I stepped over. I discarded the cigarette, and then I leaned down and put my elbow on the sill. I scanned the backseat out of paranoia. Blum was alone in the car. He was smiling.

He showed, as he hadn't done all night, a sense of humor. "Mr. Pembrook, please get in or someone will think I'm soliciting you." He laughed. It was a low, nice laugh, not unkind.

In a way, I thought, *that's exactly what you're doing.* It was no matter. I trusted Blum well enough. Only good things came from interactions with him, so I opened the door and got into the passenger seat. With the stream of heat from the dashboard vents, I began to thaw. I put my hands near one as if it were a flame.

Blum drove a block and pulled into the parking lot of a law office. The place was dark with no lights nearby. He shut off the motor, and, in a few seconds, we were together in the darkness. The car was warm and smelled like leather. Blum looked at me. His seat creaked.

"What's this about?" I asked.

"Orders from Mrs. Blum," he admitted. "Although I was easy to sway. I was on my way to The Prichard to see you. I was going to come up to your room and bother you there. This will do, though."

I spread my magazine on my lap just for something to do. I smoothed out the cover.

He wasted no time. "First this," he said. He reached into the backseat and fetched a bundle. He handed it to me.

It was a heavy topcoat of navy wool.

"It's very lightly used," he said, apologizing. "It'll be quite large on you, I imagine, but it's all we could do with no shops open."

Taken aback by the gesture, a swell of gratitude and embarrassment hit me. "Thank you," I said. Judging by the touch, the coat was expensive.

Blum put up his hand to stop me. "Genevieve and Audrey and Adeline wouldn't stop going on about how you weren't wearing a coat tonight. They were afraid you'd catch your death. Good Lord, if they'd known you were out walking in it, too." He shook his head, imagining the outrage. "All the same, it'll hold you over until you get something better."

I unfolded the coat. The buttons had the texture of horn. "It's very kind of you," I said. "Thank you. Truly."

"Moreover, Mr. Pembrook, Genevieve and I would like you to stay at our home as a guest."

"That's generous of you, Mr. Blum, but I have a room. You don't need to do all this for me. Don't think me ungrateful."

He nodded. "We'd like for you to stay with us instead. We have plenty of space. We'd like to be near you and talk to you. I can offer a stipend as long as you'd care to stay."

Temptation was there, but it wasn't strong. I leaned back in my seat and looked out the window. No traffic passed. A gust of wind buffeted the car.

"This is about your son, isn't it?"

He swallowed. "We have a lot of questions about Charlie," Blum said. "That's certainly part of it. But there's more to it than that, Mr. Pembrook."

I looked at him again and felt a trace of guilt. How could I not? I'm not an ogre. "Is it just me, or will Anna and Ruben be staying, too?"

"It'll be you alone. I trust Mr. Graf, and Anna seemed kind, but, of the trio, you have the talent. We knew it instantly. I knew when I greeted you at the door. You have an aura, Mr. Pembrook. Genevieve is very gifted at deciphering what a man's aura means. After the way you connected with Charlie, there was no doubt in our minds. We felt as if you were a childhood friend of Charlie's." Blum touched the steering wheel, as if nervous. It was strange to see a powerful man behave in such a way, to fawn, to bestow gifts. "I never had that feeling with Millard Hines," he said. Self-consciously, he removed his glasses and cleaned the lenses with his lapel. "My wife says…." He stopped and hesitated. The darkness hid crimson. "You mustn't think this preposterous," he warned. "You truly mustn't."

"It's hard to shock me," I said.

"Genevieve says that…. Well, you see, she is what is called a Theosophist. Are you familiar with Theosophy?"

"Vaguely," I said. You don't come across Theosophists as often as Spiritualists in the business, yet they're out there. They're fringe. The name means something like "God Knowledge," which sums them up well enough. "I've met them, and I know some names. I know about Madame Blavatsky."

Pleased, he said, "That's correct. Helena Blavatsky, yes. Genevieve is a follower. She has gathered a sect here." He replaced his glasses.

"Only Mrs. Blum? Not you?"

"Let's say I'm on the fence. Genevieve and her group put a great deal of stock into a figure named the Count of St. Germain. Do you know about him?"

I didn't. I'd never heard the name, but I didn't want to tip my hand. I wanted to keep all advantages within reach, so I said nothing.

"He was born in Atlantis 12,000 years ago." Blum paused

and let that land. He watched for my reaction. "The Count of St. Germain only revealed himself to the world a couple hundred years ago. He was in France at the time. Old Regime France. You were not killed during the Revolution like Genevieve first thought. She's had time to meditate on that since you left."

I made no face and offered no reaction. Inside, however, I wondered why people so intelligent, cultured, and successful believed in things so batshit crazy. It was insanity, but no more than the zealous believer in a divine Jesus. The Blums inspired pity, regardless. Rich people get arrogant in their opinions, and they can get bored. When they settle on something fringe like this, hucksters like me reap the reward. It's easy to despoil them when they're bastards, but it makes it harder when they're kind. The Blums were very kind people. They meant well.

Blum spelled it out for me. "She believes that you may be an incarnation of St. Germain." He was, I gauged, sincere. This wasn't tongue-in-cheek. There was no punch line. "Whether you realize it or not," he continued. "She would like you to undergo hypnosis at some point if you're unaware of your previous histories. We work with a wonderful hypnotist. Or do you already know your past?"

"I'm not certain I'm ready to reveal anything." I said, frowning so that I wouldn't break character and smile. I took on the "contemplative gloom" that Graf had advised.

Blum watched me, somewhat crestfallen by the refusal. Genevieve would be displeased with such news. "Will you stay with us, Mr. Pembrook?"

"Not yet. Soon, perhaps. I need time to think."

"We're not a threat to you. We would never expose you to anyone who would harm you. And," he added, hedging his bets, "if you don't care to reveal such a thing, then we won't force the matter. If we're unworthy, then we will accept that. I promise. We'd still like you to speak to Charlie whether you admit to being St. Germain or not."

Admit. He was convinced.

I shook his hand. I don't know why, but it felt like a heavy gesture that the Count of St. Germain would favor. I'd have to learn about St. Germain. In the back of my mind I was thinking, *perhaps the library in town has a book on the Count.* I needed to see what I could learn before speaking with Blum again. I thought of some French phrases I could use on the couple. I had some knowledge of history, too. Although my mind stirred, I said nothing more on the matter.

"Would you like me to drive you to the hotel?" Blum asked.

"It's just a few more blocks," I said. "I'd like to clear my head. I'll walk."

"I'm sorry if you feel exposed," Arthur Blum said. He lowered his voice. "In every way, Mr. Pembrook, we are believers. In every way."

I nodded. "I'll be in touch," I said. "Very soon. Thank you for the gift."

I opened the door and got out. I slipped into the coat and thanked him again. I was twenty feet away, wrapped in wool, before Blum started the Chrysler again. He didn't try to coerce me, and he didn't follow. He pulled onto Sixth Avenue and moved in the opposite direction. He went home to Genevieve, who no doubt waited on word from him with bated breath.

Good Christ, I thought, *12,000 years old. These people.*

When I was a block away from the hotel, the speed had cooled down and leaden fatigue had settled in its place. The warmth of the coat made me even more tired. My thoughts were muddy. Given a bed, I'd crash without another thought of Blum, St. Germain, Charlie, Dominic, or Girotti. I was eager to get inside, but I paused on the sidewalk when a shape beneath The Prichard's awning caught my eye. Intuition told me to take a step backward rather than forward. The street alone separated us. I questioned whether the shape was a man or just a shadow that looked like a man. Regardless, I'd stopped before revealing myself. I threw away the remainder of a cigarette so that I wouldn't glow orange in the dark. I moved farther from the light and watched. Quiet gathered around me. My eyes adjusted.

It was a man. He was short and bulky with slacks pulled up to his chest. He coughed, and I realized how close we stood. We could've shouted at one another. A thought struck me, a feeling of recognition, but I couldn't accept it. I had to see more. The man paced like he was impatient, perturbed, or a combination of the two. He kept his hands in his pockets. The light caught his face, and I saw clearly.

It was Anna's boyfriend, Wendell Marsh.

I woke up fast. My head swam with fear. *He's here to kill us,* I thought. I battered myself with that type of thinking: *He's going to kill Anna and Graf, and then he's going to kill me, too. He's psychotic, goddamnit, and now he has a reason to do what he's wanted to do all along.* I hadn't hurt him as badly as I'd thought. I imagined he'd still be confined to a hospital bed. I'd cracked his skull. Either I'd imagined that or Marsh was a man possessed. Perhaps he'd be standing here now even if Anna had shot him. Adrenaline put a tremor in me. I steadied my hands by rolling the magazine.

Headlights coming up 9th Street illuminated him fully. Marsh wore a fedora low on his brow. The car pulled up and stopped on the street in front of The Prichard, pulled between my sightline and Marsh. That puzzled me. I gripped and coiled *Screenland* until the magazine was a bar in my fist. The car was a Mercury Montclair, teal and cream with whitewall tires. Marsh stepped up to it. The son of a bitch smiled and said something I couldn't hear. I expected a gun to come out and fire to flash from the muzzle. Instead, Wendell Marsh opened the door and crowded into the passenger seat beside Graf and Anna. He wasn't coaxed, nor was he forced. He did the action willingly.

Graf, apparently, wasn't finished for the night. With three riders now, the Mercury pulled away from the curb, rolled through a red light, and turned right onto Sixth Avenue.

From my perch in the shadows, I watched until the taillights were gone. I was confused, mad, and sick. The last three days washed over me. An afflux of blood ran to my ears. It felt like standing in the tide.

CHAPTER FIFTEEN

Feeling cold and unable to sleep, I slid a chair nearer to the wall unit: a cast-iron radiator painted white. Welcome heat pulsed out with a hiss and thump. The paint on the radiator was beginning to flake. I parted a loose petal of white with the tip of my shoe. I was damn tired of being cold, so I hovered over the thing like a miserable cat. The room's single window stood above the heater. I had no lights on, so I kept the curtains pinned back.

Being able to watch the street on one side, and having the door double locked on the other, gave me a false sense of security, but I had to take what I could get. I was up for anything that would brace me. I needed courage to think and move, but I didn't feel much bravado. Whatever Arthur Blum had inspired in me had vanished. I wasn't made for fighting. I did what I had to do sometimes, like with Marsh, but I was never one for playing macho. I was scared, and I'd admit it to anyone who cared to know. I chain-smoked and drank gin from a dirty glass. My magazine lay on the mattress unread. Acutely, I missed life at the Marley Caldwell. Given the chance, I'd go back and shoot down Anna and go on with my ratty life. That was fantasy, though.

My radio, perched on the sill, played low, bringing the

comfort of noise to the room. A station for insomniacs and watchmen aired a call-in show. The smug host talked about everything local, national, international, and galactic. The man had opinions. Some people called in to argue with him, and some people called to agree. One caller who owned a police scanner phoned every time something went down with Huntington's finest. This occurred about once an hour. He called in for things as low on the spectrum of entertainment as traffic stops, but his vocation could go from dull to electrifying fast. He called himself Bob, and he was the highlight of the program. He sounded like an old man. A wife beating call, about halfway through the night, really got Bob and the host blabbing. That conversation had tentacles and ran for the better part of an hour. Others called in to give their two cents on women working outside the home. I listened mindlessly, catching snippets, but my thoughts remained elsewhere. Both the show and my mind ran all night long.

It was toward the end of the show, around 5am, when Bob, the scanner rat, called in a final time.

"Bob, welcome back," the host said. "What do you have for us?"

Bob was breathless now. He hadn't had a reaction like that all night. He couldn't contain his excitement. That drew me out of my thoughts. I put my feet on the floor and leaned forward to hear over the radiator. "If only this had come in three hours ago it'd taken your show off the rails, Mark. Somebody just found a body."

"You're kidding. Where?"

"Ritter Park. He ain't a wino, either. He got it by gunshot to the head. Two shots. He was just lying in a ditch by the playground. Someone made a half-hearted effort to cover him with leaves. Nice clothes, one of the boys said. Okay, okay.

Hold on." Static from the scanner blared behind the caller. It was like nails against a chalkboard.

Transfixed, I exhaled a cloud of smoke.

"They got an ID. He had cards on him. They're coming over with that now. Hold on." Bob listened more. "It's a name anyhow. That's something."

"Well out with it, Bob. What is it?"

"An Italian."

I didn't have to listen after that point to know the name, but I listened anyway. My gut knew.

"Mario Girotti. A well-dressed man named Mario Girotti with two gunshot wounds in Ritter Park."

"Anything else?"

Bob listened. "He didn't have any money on him. One of the boys mentioned that." Dead air passed. "That's all for now, I suppose. That'll get us talking tomorrow, won't it?"

"It certainly will," the host said. "This just isn't the character of our town. Think of the symbolism of the playground. Think of the juvenile delinquency that plagues our country. Folks, has it arrived in Huntington?" He went on, speculating about Mario Girotti. He weaved a tale that was far from the truth. Journalistic integrity be damned.

I leaned back, shell-shocked. *What in the hell is going on*? I thought. I gripped my glass until my hand trembled. No satisfying revelation dawned on me. *That could've been me out there.* I tried to collect myself, and I tried to be reasonable. *Graf wouldn't have connected me to Arthur and Genevieve Blum if he'd wanted to kill me.* That was something I'd been telling myself all night. It was my one glimmer of hope. *If Graf wanted me dead, I'd be dead right now in Cincinnati. Anna wouldn't have come to me like she did. And I wouldn't have gone with her.* Then a hobgoblin of an idea struck me, one I'd suppressed until now. *What if Marsh had simply screwed up that first night? What if he'd been there after me and not Anna? I'd gotten lucky with him. That was no secret, but, goddamn, it could've been a surprise. If that first hit hadn't landed, there's no telling what would've unfolded.*

It was two hours before sunrise when I decided: I'd find dirt on Anna and Graf, enough to fortify me if caged, and then I'd be on a bus out of Huntington by noon. I'd start with whatever Greyhound had leaving westward, and then Phoenix would be my final destination.

I drank more gin, had a cigarette for breakfast, and then got dressed. I had a big idea, but I needed help from Dominic to pull it off.

CHAPTER SIXTEEN

I stood on the sidewalk, shivering beneath the wool top-coat, until Dominic emerged from the darkness on the opposite side of 9th Street. He walked the same route I'd taken the night before. In fact, I now stood where Marsh had been standing. There wasn't any traffic, so Dominic crossed over without permission of the light. He wore a tattered jacket that didn't match the pressed uniform beneath. He looked fresh and scrubbed, and his breath escaped in small bursts of frost. He wore black leather gloves.

Before he'd even stepped on my side, I said, "I need your help, Dom."

I must've looked like a tuberculosis case or junkie to him: I'd been high and crashed three times in twelve hours, and I'd been sitting in the dark all night. I had no color save for my puffy red eyes. To say I appeared like death warmed over was an understatement. The sodium light from the street lamp didn't do me any favors. Dominic was shocked to see how ghastly I looked. I was Jekyll and Hyde to him.

"Are you kidding, Royce? What are you doing up?" He pulled up his sleeve and checked his watch. It was close to 5:30am.

"I need your help," I repeated.

"Fine. With what?" Dominic took me by the arm and led me inside. Lights behind the glass doors glowed orange. Walking into the hotel was like entering an open mouth. I wanted free of The Prichard. "Let's get where it's warm. God, it's early, man. How do you have so much energy? What are you on?"

Inside, we walked toward the restaurant. Dominic discarded his jacket and gloves and pulled out a ring of keys. This was just another morning to him. My presence was an interruption. Our energies couldn't have been more oil and water at that point.

"You short on funds?" he asked. "What's the problem?"

The lobby was empty save for a clerk and maid at the front desk. She was sitting on the counter with her legs dangling, crossing and uncrossing to the clerk's delight. The two were absorbed in one another. Dominic waved at them and said, "Morning." They didn't care about his arrival, just like they hadn't cared about me traipsing through the lobby earlier.

Quietly, I said, "I need you to let me into someone's room."

That brought about the first change in Dominic's attitude. "Why the hell would you want to do that? You know you'd put my ass on the line by doing that."

He unlocked the restaurant, and we walked inside. He left the lights off. It was cool, and fried olive oil and French onion soup hung in the air. The cloying aroma didn't mix with no sleep and a stomach full of gin. I almost gagged and nearly released my feelings on the floor. I gathered myself while Dominic got busy. Chairs were stacked on tables all around the dining room floor. He moved about, taking down the chairs. I followed after him.

"Because I'm afraid, and I need it," I said.

He stopped and looked over a table at me. "You aren't

kidding me, are you? Because if this is a gag it ain't funny. I don't want to be drawn into no shit either. My ass would get fired for a thing like that. Man, I barely know you, you understand."

"Do I look like I'm screwing with you? I'm a goddamn mess, aren't I? Look at my hands. It looks like I got a god-damned palsy."

He hesitated, sighed, and then said, "Whose room? Tell me that much."

"Ruben Graf."

"Oh, hell no. No." He took down another chair, turned his back on me and then turned around again. "Mr. Graf? Royce, man, you've lost your mind."

"I need you to help me. I'm asking you."

Dominic laughed, but it was nervous rather than mocking. He scratched his head, and one of the greased black strands fell over his forehead. "Why him of all people? He's one guy that could do something about it. Have you seen the thug he travels with? He'd say one word and have me done for."

"I'd rather not say why just yet. I'll tell you everything, though. Soon. You have to trust me. Please, Dom."

He pushed back the hair from his face. He tried to play it cool, but I had him worried deep down. He was shaken, and I felt guilty for that. "You're getting to be a pain in the ass, Royce." He smiled to offset the remark. He meant it and didn't mean it at the same time. It was one of those things. "When do you need it done? Tonight when they head out?"

"I can't wait that long. It needs to be now."

He scoffed. "He and that girl are probably up there asleep right now," Dominic said. "You can't just tiptoe around the bed and snoop. You ain't Perry Mason." He shook his head and went back to taking down the chairs. We walked all around the dining room.

I thought some more. "When's the restaurant opening?" I asked.

"About an hour."

"Then that's what I'll do. I'll tell them I got big news, and I'll ask them to meet me down here for breakfast. Then I'll be a little late to arrive."

"Sounds flawless. Pristine. How about I beg one of the maids to stand outside their door and beat a frying pan? That way we can be sure they're awake to get your invitation. Man, you're high as hell on something, and I don't want any part of it. You're off your rocker. That's what it is."

"I'm not high on anything."

He made a face. "Don't give me that. You smell like a saloon, Royce. I ain't judging, I've been there, but you do. The stuff's seeping out of your pores."

I slammed down one of the chairs. The noise reverberated against the gold leaf dome, all the way out to the clerk and maid. "I think he's going to kill me," I said. Exaggerated or not, that's as plain as I could make it. I paused and let the weight settle. "Don't make a face, Dom, I'm not paranoid. You remember the detective who left a message for me yesterday? Girotti?"

Dominic nodded. He was looking around, worried that I'd brought attention from his coworkers, which I had. Thankfully, nobody appeared at the door of the restaurant.

"Cops found his body at the park this morning. He'd been shot."

That upset him. Jarred, he asked, "How do you know that?"

"It's already news on the radio. It'll be in the papers this evening." I walked around the table, emphatic. "Girotti said he had dirt on Anna Vogel. That's the woman up there with Graf. He said he had something on her, and he wanted to talk to me about it. And now he's dead. I never got to talk to him."

"I don't like any of this," Dominic said.

I wanted to grab him and shake him after an inane thing like that. "Who in the hell does, man? What kind of thing to say is that?"

"I mean I don't want involved." He stared at me, jaw set, prepared to hurt me. "You're scarin' the hell out of me now."

"I don't want you involved either. I want you to stay as far from it as you can. I just need you to unlock a door for me. That's it. Unlock a door and play dumb about it. There's nothing else."

He bit his lip and looked at the floor. "That's easy enough to say."

"And then you know what you're going to do?"

"What?"

"You're going to leave this shit hole town with me. We're going to get on a bus and go out west. Go out to Phoenix. I want you to start over with me. You're going to up and quit and leave."

"You're making a hell of a lot of assumptions." He tried to be tough, but he cracked a smile. "The plan doesn't sound half bad, though."

"It's warm in Phoenix," I said. "It's like a vacation year 'round."

We both laughed.

"You just need me to unlock his door?" Dominic asked. "Is that really all?"

"That's all. I'll even lock it again on my way out."

"And when are we getting on this bus to Phoenix?"

"Before your shift is over."

"That a promise?

"That's a promise."

"You got me scared, Royce."

"I know that, and I'm sorry."

"Scared for you, I mean."

• • •

There was no need for the maid with a frying pan. Around first light that morning, I went up to the tenth floor and made my way down the hall to Graf's room. Everything was quiet, and I was a ball of nerves. I put on a face. That was the best talent I had, after all. I'd showered and shaved. My hair was combed back and wet. I was rotten on the inside, but I looked like I had it together on the outside.

I had my hand cocked, ready to knock, when an inner voice said, *just gather your things and leave. Take Dom and go. So what if you never learn what's going on? Why does that matter to you?* I didn't know the answer as to why it mattered, but I knew that it mattered. I was tired of being in the dark just like I was tired of being cold. Perhaps it was a matter of principle. I struck that one. A man like me couldn't really plead principles. Maybe I was just curious to the point of foolishness. Or it could have been none of those things. It'd been a hell of a long time since I'd been in trouble, so maybe it was just time for me to step into some. Perhaps I was mad.

There it was: ego.

Regardless of why, I brought my hand down and knocked a staccato burst.

I'd expected to stare at my shoes and wait, but Anna opened the door like she'd been standing on the other side the whole time. She looked me up and down. I knew by her red eyes that she hadn't been asleep that night. She'd taken enough pills to get a pharmacy started, so the consciousness surprised me.

"Don't you look dapper," she said. "You look like you're here to ask our son on a date."

"Is Ruben awake, too?"

"What of it?" Her mouth hung open. Lines, a mix of age and hardship, spread from her mouth and eyes. She was wearing a blouse and no pants. "You got a cigarette? I'm fresh out."

I gave her a cigarette and lit it. "I got big news," I said. "About the Blums."

She frowned and took a drag. "Huh?"

"How about I treat the two of you to breakfast? My treat this time. Would you meet me downstairs?"

Anna rested her head against the doorjamb. Her mascara was smeared. "Apparently, you had a shorter night than me." She began to shut the door.

I grabbed it. "I insist. It's big news for you, too. He thinks we're a team."

"Ruben won't like that he talked to you and not him."

Graf heard his name this time and came shuffling. He stood behind Anna and looked me over. He wasn't wearing a shirt. I noticed a jagged knife scar on one shoulder and a bullet scar on the other.

"What's this about Arthur Blum?" he asked. He used his fingers like a comb to push back his hair.

"Your cash cow came through with a bigger idea and bigger offer than you'd planned. And better than that, it's his wife who's pushing it."

Graf pointed at me and said, "You know what happened to Hines. Don't forget it."

"That's why I'm standing here. I won't do anything under

the table or behind your back. Come down to the restaurant, and I'll tell you about it."

He sighed. "I could use some coffee," he said. He shook away his haze and tried to think. His brain was in high weeds.

"Half hour?" I asked.

Anna looked up at Graf (he had half a foot on her). He nodded.

"We'll get dressed and meet you down there," Anna said. With that, she shut the door.

CHAPTER SEVENTEEN

On the seventh floor, I leaned against the wall beside the elevator and waited. A trio of men in suits, salesman types scrubbed clean, shuffled out of their rooms and headed downstairs. I declined the attendant's invitation to join them on the elevator. The businessmen looked at me as if I were a bum, and then they were gone. My nerves were working on me, but I couldn't do much about it. I just stood there, rigid, smoking, waiting for a word from Dominic. A young couple came out of their room and waited by the elevator and looked at me the same way the salesmen had looked at me. I ignored them, studying my watch. They got on the elevator and were gone.

Finally, a couple minutes before 7am, the elevator opened, and Dominic stepped out rather than the usual attendant.

He wasted no time. "Get in. They just got down to the lobby."

I stepped inside the elevator. Dominic worked the panel and took us up to the tenth floor. We left the elevator there with the doors open and started down the corridor. The hallway wasn't empty. A man stood toward the middle of it with his hands in his pockets. For a moment, I thought it was Wendell Marsh, and my heart stopped. He turned out to be another business type. He didn't make eye contact as we passed.

With a few quick movements, Dominic unlocked Graf's door. "Be fast," he whispered.

I nodded and checked my watch again. "I'll be downstairs in ten minutes."

This was where his role ended. I wouldn't have allowed Dominic to accompany me inside the room even if he'd wanted to do so. Thankfully, the guy in a suit started toward the open elevator, and Dominic had to rush to join him. That left me alone completely. I opened Graf's door and stepped inside.

A cloying stench, an unventilated, somewhat rancid tangle of pomade, perfume, sweat, unwashed sheets, and rotten food, filled the suite. It wasn't pleasant. I switched on the lights and made haste. I'd expected an elegant setup, a few steps above the room I inhabited, yet that's not what greeted me. Rather than a classy mix of furniture, art prints, and thick carpets, I found a disheveled mess: dirty clothes thrown around, sheets of newspaper spread out to soak up spills, cigarette stubs on the carpet, burn marks on the furniture, empty bottles on the floor, and mummified food on the coffee table. The rot got inside my sinuses. Graf, I concluded, had an agreement that housekeeping would steer clear of the room. He and Anna were slobs. One would have to excavate a space on the furniture just to have a seat. Not a square foot was uncovered by debris. The curtains were drawn so that no light got inside, and that made the whole scene even gloomier. A television, left on with the volume down, played a news program. Grey tones of light fell on an overturned vase of cut flowers, dead carnations. The water had poured out and dried hard.

The chaos of the room complicated things. I wanted to find

some type of correspondence, anything between Graf and Anna before we'd arrived in Huntington, but I hadn't expected the suite to be an overflowing garbage can. In my imagination, there'd be a neat bureau with a row of pigeonholes stuffed with papers. I'd sift through them, find what I wanted, and take off. There was nothing like that in the room, and the clock was ticking. I'd already squandered two minutes.

I went into the bedroom, which was even more of a mess than the living room, and I canvased a chest of drawers. All the clothes were out on the floor, so the thing was mostly empty. I found a few postcards, receipts, and junk mail. The mail was a mix of documents where Graf attempted a con with a Diners Club card.

A cold feeling of failure and futility came over me. I was striking out. I kept panic from rising to the surface, checked my watch again, and then went for the closet. A goddamn sawed-off shotgun and a handful of loose shells lay on the floor. The sight jarred me, exciting dread and putting an itch in my spine. My heart was in my throat. A metal fireproof box waited behind the shotgun. I went to my knees on the gummy carpet and tried to open the box, figuring, if they were smart, I'd need to locate a key. The box was unlocked.

Five minutes now.

This was something. The box held a few rings: two that looked like the gaudy kind Millard Hines wore the night we'd met and an engagement ring so expensive it wobbled your knees (it held a diamond that someone like Genevieve Blum would own). There was also a chain of gold, a mix of real pearl earring sets (I rolled one and felt the flat imperfections), and a marriage certificate. I picked up the latter and held it away from the shadows. Dated 1952, the Hamilton County courthouse in Ohio had issued the document.

Ruben Graf and Anna Vogel were married. And the marriage wasn't brand new.

Why lie about something like that? I thought. *Why start with a lie about Wendell Marsh?*

I thought about what this meant and let it settle unanswered. I'd have to consider implications later. Time ran low. Newspaper clippings, like the lining of a birdcage, lay beneath the jewelry and certificate. Feeling the suspense of dwindling time, I lifted each. The first, aged yellow and made brittle with quarter folds, jolted me. A date on the back read February 19, 1950. I took a long breath then. It was the *Caveat Emptor* article that Frank O'Shaughnessy had written about me. I scanned through the piece, despite myself. I was surprised that, even though six years had passed, I remembered every cute phrase, every sentence, every jab, every accusation. It was so fresh that it felt I'd read the article only the morning prior. An old pain, the heat of scarring humiliation, washed over me.

Pembrook, furthermore, is the scion of a toppled dynasty, O'Shaughnessy wrote. He had to go there. He had to point that out. It mattered to him, and it mattered to his audience. My face went red and grew warm as I scanned the words. *His grandfather is Wilhelm Pembrook. Remember him, folks? He was once a baron in the soda industry and a name as familiar as Andrew Mellon in the 1920s. The scandals of Wilhelm Pembrook and Eva Pembrook, his daughter, are familiar to most of that generation who dwelled on the eastern seaboard, so I won't recount them here. Let it suffice to say that Eva Pembrook, Royce's mother, remains in prison to this day. Wilhelm molders in the grave Eva made for him. To the point: Royce Pembrook uses a gilded past and elite education to ingratiate himself with wealthy families. Typically, these are families that have lost a loved one (especially sons during the late war). It is as deplorable and predatory as it sounds. His charlatan act is transparent for those not blinded by grief. This writer had an associate attend two of Pembrook's séances. Here's how the spider weaves his web ....*

With the wound reopened, I placed the article in the box. I shuffled through what remained. A few were ephemera of little interest (one being a carnival advertisement with Anna's name underlined in pen). The freshest articles of the set, however, revealed a great deal to me. One was dated September 18, 1956, and it, like all the previous, had been cut from the *Cincinnati Enquirer*. It was another *Caveat Emptor* piece, less than a month old, by Frank O'Shaughnessy.

It was an exposé about another fake medium in the city, a pet peeve for the journalist. The article was about Anna Vogel.

It is with great pleasure, dear readers, that today I shed light on a predator in a niche yet slimy business. The tendrils of this vocation violate our most important citizens. O'Shaughnessy's tone was more purple and comical than it had been with my article six years prior. Maybe he had changed with age, or maybe he didn't take Anna seriously. As if it were a feature slated for the comics, the subtitle read: *The Malfeasance of Madam Vogel.* The indictments, though, were damning rather than humorous. He proceeded to ruin Anna's ability to ply her trade with a mix of quips, multiple insinuations about a background in prostitution, and direct accusations. He detailed, like he had done with my article, how Anna duped her clients, particularly the wealthy widows upon whom O'Shaughnessy heaped outrage and compassion. *Caveat Emptor, citizens, Buyer Beware,* he ended the article. Ruben Graf's name did not appear in print, I noticed.

The *Caveat Emptor* article was a stepping stone to the final piece. The two articles were linked. This column, razored with precision, had a date scrawled on the back: October 8, 1956. It was, I realized, only two days old. It was a hasty, quick piece, shoved into a morning edition at the last minute. The contents were brief and lurid.

Famed Journalist and Socialite Slain, the headline read.

Frank O'Shaughnessy, a favorite of readers of the Enquirer, *and a member of fashionable society in the Queen City, whose* Caveat Emptor *series was syndicated throughout the state of Ohio and beyond, was found murdered last night in his stately home. Mr. O'Shaughnessy was killed by gunshot in what police are labeling an "execution" style assault. Authorities have released no further information on the crime and no further information on suspects, although it is difficult for the editorial staff at the* Enquirer *to believe that Mr. O'Shaughnessy fomented a single enemy, let alone a list of them. It is rumored that the O'Shaughnessy family have engaged the services of a private detective to expedite the process of investigation. When reached, the family did not provide comment.*

Frank O'Shaughnessy was a crusader for good in this community. Details about services and interment are forthcoming.

I could have pored over the articles for another hour, but one reading told me enough. An image of intentions crystallized. I had an idea what Mario Girotti meant when he claimed Anna was setting me up to take a fall. I got it: all of this had to do with Frank O'Shaughnessy. He had been murdered the night Anna came running into the Marley Caldwell.

For the time being, I couldn't dwell on the matter. I was down to two minutes, so I had to move. The thought of Graf waiting at a table in the restaurant, growing more perturbed, spurred me. I put away the certificate and articles and rearranged the contents as I had found them. The box clinked shut in the quiet room.

I took out a cigarette and put it in my mouth but stopped before lighting. It was all out of nervous habit. I put the cigarette away again and hurried through the living room, navigating the refuse. I was confident I'd left no signs of entry. In that way, the mess was a blessing. I could take a piss on the wall, and no one would notice.

Well, so long anyway, Anna, I thought. *It was a noble effort.*

I got to the door and checked my watch again. I couldn't just run off. That would make Graf suspicious, and I needed him to think I was dumb to things. I had to play along and tell him about Arthur Blum. Once we left the restaurant and parted, I'd pack and leave. This would buy me the most time. I'd be several hours away before he knew I was gone.

I'd go downstairs and apologize for being late. I already had an excuse planned. A telephone call caught me off guard, and I'd lost track of time. It was a simple, everyday thing. Dominic would back me up on the call if necessary.

I ran through it:

All apologies, Mr. Graf. You weren't waiting long, I hope. I'm truly sorry, you two. I mean it. Yeah, I know it's rude. It's damn rude. Here, let me order you something.

What about Arthur Blum? he would ask.

Have you heard about the Count of St. Germain?

These were plans in my head. They made sense and checked out. The details were suspicious only if you started out suspicious. Plans, no matter how complete, mean very little in the end, though. Sometimes I think idiot chaos is the force that truly governs the world. There's no designer, no plans, no pusher, just abrasive and bludgeoning chaos. You either get smashed or do the smashing. You can try to choose on which side you'll fall, and I was trying my damnedest to make choices that left me on the happier side, but really you're at the mercy of whizzing bullets, the mercy of centimeters and seconds and the whims of others. It's like a game of billiards out of control.

In that moment I thought I was directing the show, that I was fully in control, but I opened the suite's door just at the right moment to see Anna walking from the elevator, toward the room.

Another minute and I would've been out of the room with the door locked and closed, suspiciously in the hall, perhaps, but not in the room. There would have been ambiguity. One minute, perhaps even thirty seconds earlier, and that would've been the situation in which I found myself. As it was, I stood in the open doorway when I spotted Anna. She was flustered, her hands were in her purse, and her head was down. She looked up at the noise, and we made eye contact. Anna's jaw dropped. It was a momentary shock, one she managed to get on top of, but it was there in full view. I felt the same.

I stood with the door ajar. I thought about running. She'd cut loose with a blood-curdling scream if I did, and I'd be finished. The game was up for now. I had to think fast or suffer the hammer strike. It was coming down.

Anna picked up her pace and hurried forward until she stood before me. "What the hell are you doing?" she asked.

I looked at her without emotion. "I was downstairs and didn't see you in the restaurant. I came up looking for you, and the door was unlocked. I was worried. I thought you got into it with Ruben."

That didn't move her, not in the slightest. Unconvinced, she said, "What the hell are you doing, Royce?"

She inched forward, and I backed into the room. I lied some more, feigning concern for her safety, but it went nowhere.

"I come up to get coins for the paper, and I find you sneaking out of my room. Don't give me shit, Royce. What in the hell are you doing?"

I put my hands up in surrender as if I were making light of things. We were fully inside the room now, so I nudged the door closed with my shoulder. I didn't want any attention. I had the blackjack in my pocket, and I considered brutalizing her with it. Things just go through your mind. Impulses. In that short span of seconds, when self-preservation took over, I contemplated a lot of unsavory activities. I killed her ten times in ten different ways. She had me caged, and you do things you don't like when you're caged. I thought about O'Shaughnessy. I thought about Anna's capacity for deceit. A scenario with me busting open her skull went through, but I rejected it for the time being. I didn't want something gruesome on a hotel room floor. Not even Dominic could help me with that.

Standing before me, Anna looked like Mina from *Dracula* again, an image I couldn't shake, except now it was Mina with Dracula's blood in her veins, after she preferred the night to the day. Anna even wore a lace choker to hide the vampire bite.

"Okay, you got me," I said. "I'll level with you if you level with me. At least hear me out."

She laughed. It was a laugh that was hateful in normal circumstances, and it didn't change for this. "You're getting wise, aren't you? Ruben said you were getting wise." Anna bit her lip and thought. Decisions and choices weighed on her, leaving a look of consternation. "He saw it in you last night. When you were in the back seat. He can read people better than you think. He says you're an arrogant prig. He's right about that."

"Ruben's such a nice man, too. You're hurting my soul, Anna. I'm not wise to anything."

"How much did the private dick tell you? We can start there."

"Nothing. He didn't tell me anything. He never got a chance to tell me anything."

"So much for being on the level." Anna reached into her purse and pulled out the Beretta. She held the gun without aiming it. The gun just existed. That was the threat. She was relying on that fact to frighten me. She tossed her purse aside, and the contents rattled onto the floor. A tube of lipstick rolled until garbage stopped it. That got me looking into the living room, and I saw the television screen again. The news played low. A reporter was on the scene at Ritter Park.

"They're talking about your man Girotti right now," I said.

She ignored that. With the Beretta in her grip, she got meaner. "Now let's try it again, faggot."

I set my jaw. "Don't call me that. I'm just going to say it once. We aren't on irreconcilable terms yet."

"How much did Girotti tell you?" she persisted. Anna looked me over with disgust. It was a hatred she'd hidden until now. With words like the one she just used, she reminded me of my mother, Eva. Until the day I broke off contact with her, my mother was relentless with that word. She carved it into paper she wrote it so hard, with so much bitterness. She'd tried to humiliate and shame me with it, so the word had a lot of baggage for me. Not that I needed any assistance, but that connection got me seeing red. Something turned on inside me, and rage smothered fear. The gun wasn't quite so terrifying anymore. It was one of those states in which people do a stupid thing that gets them killed. Reason dries up.

Anna wasn't finished. "If you even think of going for that sap, I'll shoot you in the gut. And you'll bleed out and die right here." With the gun, she gestured at the floor.

"I never met Girotti," I said tightly. "You killed him first."

She didn't react to the accusation. My knowledge of things didn't strike her like I'd hoped. If being called a murderer didn't hit her, then there was nothing human inside. And, I realized then, Anna drew everything, all perceptions of herself, from the inside. No outside perceptions mattered. No words. She experienced nothing except the moment, the immediate sensation.

"Who let you in the room?" she ordered. "I wanna know that, too, because you ain't in this alone. I'm not so stupid as that."

My jaw was rigid. "It was unlocked."

"The hell it was. Ruben wouldn't do that if you paid him to leave it unlocked. He's a paranoid son of a bitch. You know how many times he'll get out of bed and check a lock at night? Don't kid me, Royce. Who let you in the room? Was it that fairy at the desk you flirt with? You bedding him? I thought your kind only went after young boys."

That was the one too many.

With a deft motion, I grabbed at the wrist of her gun hand. She thought I'd cower and take the trampling, because the action caught Anna by surprise. She'd been gesticulating with the gun rather than aiming it, so a mashed trigger would result in the wall getting hurt more than me. She yanked her hand back to avoid the thrust, and her elbow banged into the wall, hard. Her face went red as her arm went numb. I caught her wrist, and she struggled. I brought my other hand down and began to pry the gun loose. I ripped her fingers away from the trigger guard before she managed to fire. With my grip, I mashed the bones in her arm. The wrist bones twisted. Anna was mean, but she was also weak as a kitten. She had no weight on her frame. When things got physical, she was just a wisp. When she kicked and screamed, though, I did what I had to do. It was a matter of survival over principle.

I kept one hand locked on her wrist and got the blackjack out of my pocket with the other. The weight felt solid in my hand. I hit her once with the leather sap, hard enough that it caused her eyes to roll back. She let go of the gun and staggered from the wall. Although stunned, she kept her feet. I hadn't hit her hard enough to black out. I didn't want to brain her, not yet. I put the gun in my pocket and shoved Anna down onto the floor. She landed on her back without bracing herself. The thud shook light fixtures in the room and the room below it.

I got on my knees beside her. For a moment, I considered killing Anna. The urge to do so was inside me, and it grew strong, surging as adrenaline surged, but I checked it. The blow with the sap had vented some anger, enough to let me breathe. I watched her eyes. She was fully conscious. A knot the size of an egg grew purple at her hairline. I got on top of her and pinned her arms with my knees. In another second, she'd be fighting again. When Anna tried to move and couldn't, she kicked her legs and began to cry.

"Scream once and I'll brain you," I said. I meant it.

She bit her jaw so hard she tore loose a chunk of flesh. Her face was crimson. A swollen vein snaked down her forehead.

"You're breaking my arms," she said. She gasped in pain.

"I'll let loose, but you can't fight."

She nodded.

I freed her. Then I took out the Beretta and held it ready to fire. I aimed the muzzle at her face. I wanted her to look inside of it and think about things.

She rubbed her biceps, which were already coloring with bruises. Her face went from red to pale like she was going to vomit.

"A mess like that won't do anything for that nice dress," I said. "Better hold it in or swallow it."

She wiped away tears and tested the knot on her head with her fingertips. The size of the knot scared her, but there was no blood. "Just like a fairy to hit a girl," she said.

"Don't aim guns at people if you don't want to get hit," I said. "And don't talk like you talked. That's our new rule, and you aren't immune to what happens when you break it."

She glared.

"You're going to tell me everything. I saw you pick up Wendell Marsh last night, so I know he isn't your boyfriend, and the story about stealing his cash was bogus. That money you had was Graf's money, and he gave it willingly. I know Graf's your old man, and it's been that way for years."

Anna smirked at that.

"I know O'Shaughnessy wrote about you, and then he was dead three weeks later. I know you, or somebody with you, killed Mario Girotti. I never met him. That was honest. He told me you were trying to pin something on me, though. O'Shaughnessy, I suppose. He wanted to get me curious because he wanted my help. That's the extent of things."

Anna grimaced as she rose onto her elbow. She kept touching the knot. "Ruben will be up here any minute."

"He'll walk in on your corpse if you don't talk. I'll be in enough trouble then that it won't matter if I kill him, too. What'd Girotti have on you?"

"He'll have you strung up, and this town won't do a thing. You wanna know why? Because they're sensible people here."

"How's that?"

"They hate fairies as much as they hate reds. That's sensible."

I kept my cool. "What'd Girotti know? You better talk, Anna." I reminded her of the gun with a touch of cold metal. "This'll be worse than a bruise."

Fear made her relent. "He knew you were going down for a murder. That's what he knew. He didn't know we had you pegged for three of them. Now you can add assaulting a woman to the list. The cops will like that. It won't hurt our case a bit."

"Three?" I asked. That made my head swim, but I hid the surge of emotion. "Girotti and who else? O'Shaughnessy?"

"Millard Hines for one."

That hit me in the gut. I tried not to show it. It was getting difficult to conceal. "Newt didn't kill Hines. I was there."

She grinned. She liked seeing a man wither. It gave her strength. "No, you're right. Newt didn't kill him. You did, old boy. Millard will be found before too long. He'll wash up on the riverbank, and then you'll have two. You benefitted from Hines because it got you in with Arthur Blum. He was a rival. Like it yet?"

"Go on," I said.

"The third's more complicated. The third's the reason for everything. It's the first one." She inched into a sitting position. Her back was arched and her shoulders low. She had to peer upward to look me in the eyes. She did. "That night when you beat up on Wendell? That night where you left work and hit a bar and then there was a big gap in time where no one saw us until you ran out with Wendell on your floor? No, I better not say," she teased. "Not just yet. We can wait on Ruben to get up here. I'll let him tell you. Or maybe you'd like Wendell to tell you."

I placed the muzzle against her flesh again. "Talk."

She was silent for a moment. I kept the gun steady. "Let's just say I settled a score with O'Shaughnessy with some help from Wendell. He's good for that sort of thing. And you're gonna to take the fall for it. Not him, and not me or Ruben, but you. The other two are just dressing to make you look like a maniac. You're already a deviant, so maniac makes perfect sense. That's the long and short of it."

"Marsh killed O'Shaughnessy?" I pushed the gun harder. "Because he wrote about you?"

She nodded. "He lost Fawn Bailey for me. He turned her against me. So you, with nothing to lose, killed him for me. You had a reason to hate him, too. He did the same thing to you that he was doing to me. He's part of the reason you got sent away to Mansfield. You didn't forget that, did you? In fact, you're obsessed with him and loyal to me. I'm like your sister, and you're always standing up for me. That's why you got Hines and Girotti. That's the way I'll tell it, at least. You're out of control, Royce, and I need to turn you in for safety."

"No one would believe that." I didn't say the words with much assurance. My confidence dwindled as Anna's confidence grew. I hated that about her. She could drain a person. It was one of her chief strengths in the world.

She grew flippant, ignoring the gun. "I was a witness at each turn, old boy. Who do you think they'll believe? Me being sweet and innocent or a deviant like you?"

I had a sick feeling that Anna was correct. The police in a hick town like Huntington wouldn't believe me. They'd begin with a prejudiced notion. Anna had left me in a position with no alibi each time a murder occurred. It was a nice piece of orchestration.

A glutton for punishment, I asked, "Why me?"

Anna shrugged. "You were as good a choice as any. You had a motive with O'Shaughnessy. And maybe I got a thing against fairies, I don't know. Or maybe you being a fairy just made things easier. Wendell never liked you for that. You started with a strike against you. Too bad you ain't a Jew on top of it."

I stood and looked down at Anna.

"Now what?" she asked. Venom laced her voice. I didn't understand her arrogance. She didn't think I had it in me to kill someone. In her mind, I'd accelerated the plan by snooping, but there was already enough of the plan in place to unfold the way she liked. I was a coward and, even though I'd fight at first, I'd ultimately lie down and take the blame. I'd head to prison, and she'd head north. That was her vision.

She was wrong on all accounts.

"I'm going to burn all of you," I said. "You, Graf, and Marsh."

"You might as well turn yourself in," Anna said, unfazed. "Go find Jimmy the Cop at the bus depot again and tell him your story. He'll love that. He had a bad feeling about you, remember? Jesus, I can't imagine what he'll do when he finds out you're a fairy, too."

"Stop saying that."

"Maybe I'll tell Ruben to seek out Jimmy today and let him in on the secret. That you're fucking a man in his town. You're gonna bring down God's wrath on these poor people. You'll be hanging from a street lamp before twilight. They do that to fairies here."

I gripped the gun until my knuckles were white. "Stop

saying it, Anna." I pointed the gun at her chest. I couldn't miss from this close. The bullet would open a hole in her back.

Although she smiled and played arrogant, terror returned to her eyes. That reality helped me balance myself. I loosened my grip. I didn't kill her because I needed her to take a fall for me now. I needed Anna alive. I began stitching together a plan.

"Get up," I said. "You're coming with me."

With shaky legs, Anna stood. We went to the door, and she opened it. Neither of us said anything. I planned on taking her down the stairs to my room until I could leave The Prichard without notice. I moved the Beretta into my pocket. I didn't want anyone to see me with a weapon. When we got to my room, I planned on gloating. I'd wait there with the gun ready until Graf came knocking.

"Down the stairs," I said.

Anna stepped out into the hall with her arms at her side and her shoulders drooping. I have to give her credit for not tipping me off. She watched me and nothing else, and the sour look on her face didn't change one iota. There must have been a shock of joy upon that exit from the suite, but the feeling didn't register on her face. She was a good actress when it mattered most.

Up until the last moment, I was in control. I kept adding details to my plan. It grew larger, more intricate. Then I took a single step into the hallway and saw Graf out of the corner of my eye. It happened fast. His fist was already coming down when I spotted him. I guess he'd been there with his ear pressed, listening for the past few minutes. I couldn't say, and I never found out for certain. Perturbed, he'd followed Anna upstairs at some point. That much was clear. Poor Dominic had eaten his fingernails over the fact.

Graf wore brass knuckles. He hit me so hard, the force caused me to pivot. My ass dropped off of me with that first hit. My arms and legs quit. It was like being struck by a slab of concrete, and the sound against my skull was about the same. He grabbed me by the collar, pulled me into the room, and hit me more. He sliced my eyebrow, and blood poured down. I tried to defend myself, but Graf hit me until I stopped thinking and feeling. Everything was black. In hindsight, I think Anna came into the room and kicked me. I can't be sure. It might be a dream. Without doubt, though, she's the one who took the Beretta and blackjack from my pocket. That I remember.

The sound of running water revived me. At first, I thought I was outdoors in an idyllic field with a stream trickling near my feet. I pictured tufts of wildflowers, and I saw Anna and Graf shot through with arrows against a big, gnarled yew tree. The tree was a thousand years old, and it didn't give a damn. It even moved its branches so the sun could bake Graf into leather. It was a pleasant vision, one I'd be happy to sleep with, but it didn't last. The fleeting vision went, and now the stream swelled around me, pinging like rain, and reeking.

I creased my eyes. My face felt like earth cracking with drought. My head was like the sock of broken glass Newt had used on Millard Hines. Rather than the scenic meadow, I found myself in a room with a floor of packed dirt and cinder block walls. An opaque window as thin as a visor allowed a rectangle of light inside. The window was enough to let me know the changeover from night to day, but I wouldn't get any vitamins standing beneath it. I looked up to find Wendell Marsh with his penis out, pissing asparagus and beer on my shoes and slacks. The gap between reality and dream was a "this is what you want, and this is what you get" level of disparity.

Anger isn't the right word for the way I felt. My brain was

too bruised to be mad, per se. I just watched until Marsh finished his business, which he eventually did. He shook a drip from his member and put it away. There wasn't enough dick there to write my name on, just a stub.

"When you gotta go, you gotta go," Marsh said.

I hoped he hadn't been saving up that quip, but I figured he had.

I'd bitten off a sliver of tongue, I found then. Exploration gave me a lot of unpleasantries to discover. The sliver left an open sore on the edge, and the wound had my tongue distended to twice its normal size. It was more embroidery in the tapestry of agony I experienced. My face was swollen, encrusted with blood. My nose was broken, smashed, and I couldn't breathe through it without immense pain. A cut the size of a mouth gaped at my eyebrow. The pain made me sick.

With the heavy tongue and bruised jaw, I didn't say very much, not clearly anyhow. Words came out as thick sounds, muddled. I watched Marsh, though, and breathed with exhalations that sounded like hisses from the back of my throat. I belonged in a hospital.

Marsh buckled his belt, hitched his pants up to his chest, and then tucked and straightened his shirt. With the light behind him, he was mostly shadow. Without fine details, Marsh looked like a cube of granite, wide as he was tall.

"It's been a long time, Royce. How goes it?"

I didn't say anything.

Marsh laughed. He had a laugh that was dry and joyless. It was more like a nervous laugh, as threatening as cracking knuckles.

"I gotta get somethin' off my chest," he said.

He knelt beside me. I had an acute sense of things: his cologne was cheap and heavy, and it masked body odor; his

Cuban collar shirt had burgundy stripes. A scab covered his bottom lip where he'd bitten it during our first encounter. With his massive knee close to my head, he could come down with that thing and end my life if he wanted. He'd pop my head like a grape.

He said, "I gotta know that you know something or I ain't gonna be happy. It's hurtin' my sleep. Understand?"

My eyes weren't open enough to communicate anything, so I looked like a pile of unresponsive flesh to him. I watched him and breathed loudly through my mouth.

"A few nights ago, when I was at your place, that was a lucky hit you got in. It was pure luck. Plus, you had that thing in your hand. Okay, so it clipped me good, but it was that thing doing it and not you. Can we agree on that? I'll sleep better if we can just agree on that one thing."

I stared at him. With speech that was as slurred as it was painful, I said, "Why do you piss on everything? First my floor and now me." I don't know how clearly that landed with him, the elocution lessons my grandfather had paid for weren't on display at the moment, but it landed.

After a tick, he deciphered the muddled words.

My lips curled into a bloody smile. "How do your beds fare with this condition?"

His smile straightened, paused, then became a frown. He made some noises to mock how it sounded where my tongue was too large. Then he said, "You ain't in a position to be funny, pal. You got no room to talk if you know what I mean."

I conceded that point.

He stood again. "It was pure luck," he mumbled. "Goddamn you." Then he put his hand against the edge of his mouth and shouted, "Hey, Rube, your boy ain't dead. He's awake."

I closed my eyes and felt like going unconscious again. The

relief of such a thing didn't occur. I was wired awake, lucid, and feeling every sensation. Behind all this I had a desperate craving for a cigarette. When I recognized the craving, it gnawed at me.

The door opened, and several bodies filed down the stairs into the chamber. The small space, a root cellar, became crowded fast. They made a crown around me, and they looked down as if watching a coffin being lowered into the earth. The mood was far from somber, though. They were celebrating my return to the world. I'd scared them by being unconscious so long. My death did nothing for them. Me being dead was the end of their plans. There was no need for introductions. I recognized all of them: Newt, Graf, Anna, and Marsh, of course.

Seeing them arrayed put a picture in my mind, and the picture made me want to bang my head against the block wall. I'm not a believer, but there was something religious in the image of the moment. I was positioned to be a sin eater for everyone in the room. They'd be absolved because of me. I've read about sin eaters. I once read about a backwoods cult in Carolina who designated a young man, feebleminded, to go through a ritual every time someone in the combine passed away. This wasn't medieval. This was in the 1920s. The kid, who lived in the dark about everything, would take in all the person's sins so they'd be clean in the afterlife. He'd eat a meal that represented their bad deeds, and the food, as a rule, must be bitter. The bitterness was just one of the rules. It was strange. It reminded me of Dorian Gray when I'd read the article (it was in one of those glossy magazines like *Life*), but now I saw myself in the same role as the feebleminded child. I was about to eat some bitter food.

Graf had a suit of new clothes on and a white belt. The

polyester had a shine on it like polish. He looked cheap. Off the rack man that he was, I wasn't surprised. He said, "My, but you look awful. I got carried away."

I agreed with him.

He looked over his handiwork. There was more pride than concern in his face. He wanted Newt and Marsh to look on me with surprise, too. *See, I'm no slouch either,* the look said. *See?*

"You were out a few long hours, friend," Graf said.

"You smell like piss," Anna observed. "You're rank." She looked like a runt among the men. The knot on her head hadn't diminished. She still wore the lace choker.

I groaned. "That isn't mine," I slurred. I pointed at Marsh. "He didn't want to be alone in pissing his pants. He let me have some of his." In my mind, at least, the words were clear.

Anna and Newt laughed while Marsh glared.

"I don't think he meant to wake me," I added.

"Enough of that," Graf said. "This can go two ways, Royce. Hear me out."

Choices, I thought miserably. Despair crept into my thoughts. I didn't want to think about choices. If I hadn't chosen to sneak around in Graf's hotel room, I'd be on a bus with Dominic right now. We'd be heading west, with paranoia being the only pain I felt. I could stand looking over my shoulder. I'd promised to board a Greyhound with him before his shift ended today. Obviously, that wasn't going to happen. He thought I was just talk.

"Don't drift on me," Graf said. "Open your eyes."

I looked at him. I sat up, which made my head roll. At least my ribs and legs were in decent shape. My face and head were wrecked, but everything else was intact.

"First way is this. I got you to swallow a tiny pearl during the fracas. You probably don't recall that."

I didn't. Or maybe I did and thought it was a tooth. The edge of a memory, a sensation, surfaced. My mouth hurt too much to explore the situation, so I took his word for it.

"The pearl's down in your guts. I got $500 to give to the first man here to find that pearl. Of course, they got to get it while it's still inside you. They'll open you like a pig. It's a fun game we like to play."

This was Graf's pathetic attempt to be a tough guy. I didn't buy it. "It sounds fun," I said. "Do I have to send it back if it comes out the other way?"

He shrugged. "It's costume jewelry."

"I see."

"The second way is you turn yourself in to the cops. You march into the station and confess about Girotti and Hines. Then you tell them Anna and me can corroborate what you say. We'll suggest they look into the O'Shaughnessy case, and they'll put the pressure on you from there. It ain't quite as seamless as we'd planned before you jammed the gears, but I think it'll do."

"It might even work better," Anna proposed.

Graf didn't think so. I saw he wasn't satisfied. I saw the turmoil in his face. His worry was existential, the stress of slipping into disorder. "What do you say, friend?" he asked.

"The pearl's in my lower intestine by now. That has to make it less fun." My mouth hurt so badly that, despite my effort, tears formed in my eyes. If I'd been alone I would've broken down and sobbed. I didn't give them the pleasure. I even managed to sit up straighter.

"Just let me stomp his head in," Marsh offered.

"Five hundred makes anything tolerable," Graf said,

sticking with his tale. "Newt's done a helluva lot worse than that." He laughed.

Newt laughed. At a memory, I suppose.

"What do you say, Royce?" Graf asked again.

Marsh cut in. "How do you know he ain't gonna do an about-face?"

Anna played like she was a gun moll and said, "Simple. Newt took care of that problem, didn't you, old boy?" She had her hands on her hips like a sass queen. She felt like Dillinger's woman or the head of Ma Barker's brood. Even the knot on her head made her feel tough.

Newt spoke for the first time. He didn't like doing it, I sensed. He liked the anonymity of being the silent man in the corner. That was a form of protection for him. He did things and got paid for those things and never talked about them to anybody. He worked for more people than Ruben Graf. He was a freelancing tough. "We found where the other fairy lives. You do something we don't like, we pick him up and give him the treatment Hines got."

Marsh whistled in approval. "That works," he said.

I went cold inside. It was a solid hook, much more believable than the pearl, and, mentally, it took me from feeling defiant to feeling trapped. The thought of Newt and Marsh brutalizing Dominic tormented me. Dominic weighed 130 pounds with his shoes on. He was so thin they'd break his bones. I may not have been in love yet, but I was infatuated with Dominic, and infatuation obliterates reason. Infatuation borders on insanity. The threat to Dominic alone, plausible or not, made me curdle inside.

"We'll haul him up to the dump where we took Hines," Graf added for color. He looked over his shoulder at Marsh. He combed his blond hair with his fingers. "That good enough for insurance?"

"It checks. Big time. We credit you or Anna for that one?" Marsh asked.

"That was all Anna," Graf admitted.

Anna smiled.

I watched her.

Graf set his eyes on me again. "One more time, friend. What's it gonna be?"

I was silent. I didn't have the energy or desire to be smart anymore. I didn't care about being defiant. Without those crutches I was just a guy in a lot of pain. I looked at the ground.

Graf patted my back. He had me, and he knew it. "Think on it some more. Think it through."

Let it torment you, he should've said. *Bludgeon you. Let it pick you apart and defeat you. We'll be here when you're ready.*

Graf rummaged through the inner pocket of his sport coat and pulled out a rumpled pack of Chesterfields. He went through the labor of getting one burning and then offered it. I took the stick. There was nothing wrong with my hands, and my pride was in bad shape. The smoke made a thunderclap of pain in my mouth, but the other feeling, the salve, went deeper. I needed it. Relief spread through me like spilled ink. Graf put the pack on the floor with a book of matches.

"All right, everyone out," he said. Finally, to his satisfaction, he knew he'd hurt me. "Let him think a while. Wendell, you care you to watch him some more?" He handed over a folded twenty for Marsh's troubles.

Marsh took the cash and agreed. "Just bring me a magazine," he said. "Somethin' from Newt's stash of *Swank*."

"Fine. And for chrissakes don't piss on the floor again. Newt lives here."

"It's dirt," Marsh said. "It'll absorb."

Newt grunted. He pointed at Marsh as a warning.

With that I was alone with Wendell Marsh and my thoughts again. My reservoir stood empty. I listened to footfalls on the wooden stairs. The door opened and closed.

"That's what you get for always trying to be a comedian," Marsh was saying. He started to tell a story about some transgression I'd made when Anna and I worked the carnival circuit. Something that had made him very sore at the time, apparently.

The smoke made strange shapes in front of my face. I smoked and felt blank.

CHAPTER NINETEEN

After an hour had passed, Anna returned. She glided down the stairs with another issue of *Swank* and two bottles of beer. Marsh already had five empties and two magazines on the floor beside his chair. He was a professional when it came to guzzling beer, so I doubted that five bottles had him drunk. Five was enough to keep headaches at bay, perhaps, but not enough to entertain him. After a few unrequited jibes, he'd grown bored with me. He'd exhausted the two previous issues of *Swank*, skipping anything with words and examining the photos from every angle. He'd gone through each issue three times.

Without any talk or interest, Anna handed Marsh his things. She then stepped to the center of the floor, turning her back on him. She balanced a radio under her arm, and she hummed, discordantly, the melody of "Mr. Sandman." She watched me for a reaction.

Marsh opened one of the beers, and he watched Anna from behind. His eyes stayed on the curve of her hip, prominent beneath a tight skirt. The look was lascivious.

Time had slowed, and now I knew every inch of the chamber. Not that it did much good. The only way out of the cellar was up the stairs. The room was Spartan in its simplicity. A naked bulb hung on a wire from the ceiling. That was the only light when the sun went down. The thing danced every time somebody upstairs took a breath. Anna stood beneath the bulb now. I was on the floor with my knees pulled to my chest. Place me on my side and the position would've been fetal.

Anna pulled the cord, and the light buzzed to life with the sound of an insect. Yellow blanketed the musty cellar. A pall of smoke hung in the air like fog where I'd been working through the pack.

I looked at Anna. There was plenty to say but nothing constructive. I crumpled the empty pack of Chesterfields and tossed it toward her. The garbage stopped at her feet. She looked down at it, and "Mr. Sandman" stopped as if the needle had lifted. She had brand new shoes, I noticed, but they were department store shoes, cheaply made. Her machinations for fine living would never pan out with a hood like Graf. He was a poor man trying to be a rich man, but he didn't know anything more than middle class trash like those shoes. His utopia was carte blanche at Macy's. Anna's was even less than that: Sears, perhaps. Poor people aspire to be middle class, and they think it's rich. I wondered if she was delusional or knew that fact. I wondered if she knew how little I thought of her.

"I finished those," I said, carving into the tension. "You have anymore?"

She did. Anna tossed me an unopened pack.

I nodded my thanks. I tore off the cellophane.

"I brought you this, too," she said, taking the radio into both hands. It was a shelf unit with AM and no FM on the dial, a prewar relic, heavy duty. "I remembered how you like the noise."

Metal racks full of empty jars lined the cellar walls. I'd

studied those, too, in the preceding hour. I got the sense Newt had inherited his grandmother's house and the canning had ended with her. The jars were blue-green and ancient, from the 1910s. Anna checked the shelves until she found one where she could plug in the radio.

"Shoulda brought down a television," Marsh complained. He took a drink and looked at me. His mouth made a popping noise against the bottle's lip. I hated that. He'd been doing it like a child for the past hour, over and over. *Pop.* Silence. *Pop.* Silence. Long silence. *Pop. Pop. Pop.* "Newt's got a color TV up there." Marsh raised his eyebrows, impressed. "That's all he does when he ain't workin'. He watches *Gunsmoke.* Not that I blame him. It's about like this." He showed me the size by spreading out his arms. It was, admittedly, a big television. *How many legs did Newt have to break to earn it?* I thought.

A burst of static came from the radio speaker. Anna played with the dial until a frequency with a voice came through. A man told us we were in the middle of a "24 hour platter party," and then he blustered through an advertisement for Barbasol. Even the radio announcers had a hick twang in these parts. You could make three words out of Barbasol by the way the man pronounced it. Dion and the Belmonts followed the ad. Anna set the volume lower than her voice, and then she came toward me again.

"I suppose you find all this terribly unfair," she said. "You think I'm a monster." The gun moll attitude was gone for the moment, replaced by something coquettish.

Marsh kept watching her backside, a residual hard on from the *Swank* layouts goading him.

"Among other things," I said.

"Try to see it from my point of view, old boy. I think it'll make you feel better if you do." She was serious. She was god-damn delusional, but she was serious.

Even Marsh laughed at the absurdity. Marsh was dumb, but he wasn't mental. Anna possessed attributes of both qualities.

I stared at her shadow on the ground. As requested, I looked at things Anna's way. It took all of a few seconds to study, but still I didn't like it. The effort was noble. A question like "*don't we both matter?*" would never occur to Anna.

She persisted, and, with that slip, I knew how much my attitude bothered her. "You can at least see why we took down O'Shaughnessy, can't you? He ruined me just like he ruined you."

Marsh made the popping sound with the bottle again. It was grating. *One more time,* I thought. *One more time and I'll snap.*

I kept staring at Anna's shadow. Even in prison I'd never considered killing Frank O'Shaughnessy. He didn't mean enough to me. If I didn't care sufficiently back then, I certainly didn't care enough now. He was a pariah and a muck-raker, and we were fodder for him. If we'd had the means we could've sued him for libel, but neither of us did. That was the alpha and omega of things. I thought he was scum, but I thought a lot of people were scum. I didn't want to kill all of them. So, the answer to her question was no, I couldn't under-stand why they'd murdered O'Shaughnessy.

Something about Anna struck me then. The whole notion of her standing before me pleading her case was irrational. I got the sense that she wasn't feeling guilty about railroad-ing me, about me losing my life and going to prison again, to death row for three murders, or about Graf breaking me into pieces with brass knuckles, but the fact that I hated her for all this had her bothered. That had got in her mind, and she didn't like it. She wanted to reason with me, convince me otherwise. She'd send me Christmas cards in prison if I forgave her and said I understood. I don't know what happens to a person to turn them that way. I still don't.

I couldn't bring myself to say much to Anna, regardless. I was too morose, too angry, in too much pain. I took a drag on the cigarette instead. My mouth was over the pain of that, at least. I flicked ashes and kept my eyes on her shadow. I considered and reconsidered, measured words, and then decided. After the silence had stretched out, I said, "You're out of your goddamned mind." I could speak a trifle clearer now, although my tongue still smothered the words.

"Uh-huh," Marsh agreed. "That she is. But we love her, don't we?" He laughed and made that popping sound. That sound, I guess, was the hinge moment for everything that followed. Collectively, the three of us lost our minds.

"What gratitude," Anna said. Her chest rose and fell. She walked over to the radio and unplugged it again. So much for her act of kindness. Dion faded to nothing. Anna picked up the unit, held it over her head until I was watching (because that was the important part), and then slammed it against the floor. The radio was fine other than jumbled guts. They built things like tanks in the thirties. No plastic. She hurried back to me and made a grab for the Chesterfields, but I clutched the pack tightly to my chest.

"Get off it, Anny," Marsh said. "Go back upstairs or come over here and give me a kiss. Or have a seat on this bad boy." He gestured at his crotch. "We can entertain him like we did for Rube last night. Her asshole opens real wide, probably like yours," he said to me. "You can stick all kinds of stuff in it."

Anna turned toward Marsh.

"Don't you dare give me that look," he warned with mock

indignation. "You know Rube don't care." He winked at me and said, "Rube likes to watch. He'd watch you and your fairy slap ball to ass if you invited him. He gets off on it."

Anna uncorked. She let loose, spewing vitriol. She called me every vulgar slur she knew, and she knew quite a lot. It was a tantrum, and I got the feeling that she didn't have much control over the outburst. In my mind, though, this was a crack of daylight. She stomped, while Marsh, for real this time, grew annoyed.

Finally, he stood and grabbed her arms. "Let's get you outta that dress," he said. "Let's entertain him, Anny."

I measured things. Newt and Graf would hear Anna upstairs. They'd come down to check on the commotion eventually, but I had a minute. Although my head was destroyed, everything else worked. I looked across the floor at Marsh's empty bottles. That was a reach, but it was an option. I had another option on the rack behind me. The glass in the old jars was thick and would do damage. There was a third option: on the floor beneath the rectangular window lay a rusty crowbar. It was a forgotten tool that had been there, I assumed, for ages. Debris covered half of it, but the crook stuck out. That's all I could see. In the past hour, I'd thought many times about that piece of equipment. I liked that option best. It was ten feet away. By the time I stood, it'd only be eight.

In hindsight this was all irrational, especially with the threat it posed to Dominic, but in the moment it felt nothing except rational. It was necessary. I was caged, so I reacted like I was caged. Plenty of thoughts would have put brakes on my actions, but I thought none of them.

Marsh did two favors for me. First, he shouted upstairs. "I got her, Rube, baby. No need to come down. I'll do the comin'." He laughed at his joke.

Graf didn't answer. That, in itself, had me curious. I wondered if Graf had left, if he was upstairs at all. The shout bought time, regardless.

Second, Marsh clamped Anna's arms tighter and giggled in her ear. "Rube didn't care last night and neither did you, baby," he said. "You both liked it." He kissed her neck and touched his tongue against her earlobe. When Anna tried to jam her heel into his shin, Marsh arched his back and picked her up off the ground. When he lifted her, he turned his back on me. That was the gift. It was then that I made my move.

Unlike the proverbial cat, I moved without silence or stealth. Call it insanity or punch-drunk stupidity. Call it what you will, but I grabbed an open jar by the rim just in case I didn't make it to the crowbar, and I sprung from the floor. Anna kicked and screamed, and Marsh tried to unfasten her dress. I was halfway across the floor, two long steps, before he saw me. He was shocked at the sudden change, but he didn't hesitate. Marsh had a lot of years of fighting in him. He had instinct. He could kill me, and he didn't need a gun or knife to do so. He threw Anna to the ground, and she crashed against one of the metal shelves, toppling jars. Marsh turned and lunged.

It all happened in seconds.

Marsh had a hundred pounds on me, at minimum, and when his massive shoulder met my thigh, I went down as hard and fast as if I'd been sawed from the gallows. I'd passed by him, so he hit me from behind. I went down on my knees and then stomach. The air went out of me, forcing a gasp. The jar in my grip smashed against his chair, shattering. I was lucky the jar or scattered beer bottles didn't carve up my hands. Frankly, it was goddamn providence.

"Not this time," he was saying. "No blackjack this time, pal."

Marsh pushed down on me, his weight smashing me against the floor. He got to one knee. He punched me in the kidney so hard that I wanted to vomit. Stigmas clouded my vision. I didn't see much, but I saw the crowbar. It was within reach now. And I still had the rim of the jar, like a jagged crown, in my grip. He hit me in the other kidney, a rapid punch that followed the first, and I pissed out some blood. He didn't use his massive knee to pin me, however. That was his mistake. He didn't think I had it in me to fight back. He thought he was going to bat me around like a cat tortures a bird.

He was coming down with a third punch, this one aimed at the back of my neck, when I twisted onto my side. His fist glanced my shoulder and threw him off balance.

I palmed the rim of the broken jar, and I brought it up in a stabbing motion with enough force to disembowel a horse. The glass caught Marsh's face. It wasn't perfect, but the glass caught enough of his upper lip and chin. The flesh gave no resistance, only the pressure of recoil in my wrist. The rim slid off his face, veering upward.

Instinctively, Marsh's hands went to his face. Behind his fingers, his eyes glossed.

Anna was getting to her feet now. She screamed for Graf and Newt, for anybody.

I let go of the glass and got to my knees. I grabbed at the crowbar, catching it on the first attempt. I ripped it free from the trash.

Anna was on the stairs, halfway up, screaming, pleading for help.

Although my legs were shaky, I managed to stand. I gripped the iron, and it was cold and hard and heavy. It felt right.

Marsh tried to gather himself to fight again, but, deep down, the wound terrified him. Blood slicked his hands and covered his shirt. There was just too much of it for him not to fall victim to shock. His gritty blood was on my hands. It was everywhere.

Marsh said something, but blood in his mouth made the words unintelligible. His speech devolved into a grunt.

I looked down at him, and our eyes met. I didn't feel anything for Wendell Marsh. Call it a deficiency of character, but I experienced more emotion when I smashed a gnat. It's not a gift or a blessing, but it's a fact. I raised the crowbar and swung with everything I had inside me. He made a motion to dodge the blow, but it was a weak effort. He'd barely moved when the bar struck above his left ear. His skull gave with first contact, caving into a thin ridge along the top of his ear. Marsh went down on his face just as he'd gone down in my apartment. Despite all the beer in him, though, he didn't piss his pants this time. He'd be happy to know that.

With his face on the ground, I hit him three times. He didn't defend himself. Not once. He seized with the second blow, seized all the way down to his feet like I'd shot electricity through him, but he stopped as soon as he began. Rivulets joined and pooled behind his ear.

From beginning to end, the entire fight lasted no more than a minute.

When I looked over again, Anna was gone. The light shook from her steps on the floorboards above. She moved frenetically. Termite dust rained down around the bulb. Anna cried out for Graf. With the crowbar in hand, I started upstairs. I wasn't thinking straight. I realized that, but I acted anyway. I don't know what my intentions were. That's honest.

Newt lived in a miniature row house that edged a busy street. It was a cookie cutter place with a million more that mirrored its image. The interior of the house was smaller than most apartments, so there weren't many places to hide. I emerged from the cellar in a cramped kitchen with linoleum on the floor and a refrigerator that dated to the 1930s in the corner. Dishes and pans filled the sink. The entire space was no larger than a pantry, and it smelled of sour milk. A round table with uneven legs occupied most of the floor.

Finding no one to confront, my adrenaline waned. When that went, exhaustion and pain replaced it. My arm trembled. I had trouble controlling it. The crowbar felt heavier. My thoughts grew unclouded. The silence of the house disturbed me.

I checked the living room. There was no one in there either: just an ugly couch, a wood-encased television topped with an antenna, and enough garbage to start a landfill. A few black and white portraits in gaudy frames hung on the wall. Pork and beans and beer perfumed the air. With no heat on, a chill filled the house. Goosebumps rose on my arms and neck.

Only the bedroom and bathroom remained to be searched. My head grew clearer, and I had to question what I wanted to accomplish. The hesitation left me standing in the living room like a fool, the crowbar hanging from my grip, contemplating. I thought about torching Newt's house. That was a bug in me I'd considered a couple times before. The front windows had curtains that would do the trick. Garbage would fuel the rest. I thought about walking into the bedroom and searching for Anna. What I would do with her I couldn't say. My rage had died down. Lastly, I thought about chucking the crowbar and running out the front door. Given time, I would've done that.

Anna made the decision for me. She stepped from the bedroom with the Beretta in her hand. It was the second time she'd aimed a pistol at me that day. Unlike the first time, she kept a healthy distance between us. The gun moll was perfecting her craft, I guess. She held the gun with both hands as she aimed. Her mascara ran from crying, leaving dark half moons below her eyes. Her dress was ripped at the neck from Marsh, exposing her collarbones. Her chest heaved, and it was more from fright than fatigue.

The din of traffic came through the walls as we stood in silence, watching one another. I looked into the muzzle. I held the crowbar, and she held the pistol. It wasn't much of a match if she didn't close in on me. She was determined not to do that. I cursed myself for not searching Marsh for a gun. I hadn't even considered the need.

"Put it on the ground," Anna said finally. Cautiously, she took a step closer.

I'd already experienced a miracle by not slicing up my hands in the cellar. Anna missing a shot from so close would require divine intervention, too, and I couldn't expect two assists in one day. She aimed the gun at my stomach to increase the odds in her favor. The bullet would strike me somewhere. Then what? Where would that leave me?

I capitulated, dropping the hunk of iron. It thudded against the carpet. I put up my palms in an offering of surrender. *You should've run*, I thought. *You should've come out of the cellar sprinting*. I nixed that line of thinking. There would be plenty of time later to berate myself. The next time I had sleep to contend with, I promised, I'd be brutal. For now, I decided to be nice.

Anna ordered me to get on the couch. She pivoted to keep me in front of her. She looked like she'd learned from police in the movies.

I did as I was told. I swept away peanut shells and cool ashes and sat on the couch. The springs groaned. A piece of metal poked me through the thin cushion. Anna walked around me, pivoting, keeping distance. Her feet were shoulder width apart, and she kept two hands on the weapon. She put her back against the wall and trained the gun on me. I got the sense I terrified her. That was new. She'd been wrong every time she tried to predict my behavior. She didn't know what to think now, and that frightened her.

On the opposite side, I read Anna's thoughts. I knew her at that moment better than I'd ever known her.

"Now what?" I asked. I was weary. It remained painful to speak. Blood rushing to my head had me bleeding again. The fire in my nerves returned. I was still a horror show with a head swollen to the size of Rondo Hatton. My kidneys throbbed like something in my guts had ruptured. I grimaced. I began to reach for a cigarette, but Anna motioned with the gun until I stopped. I released a deep exhalation.

In a tight voice, one that didn't belong to her, Anna said, "We'll wait on Ruben." She was searching for her trust in him. It hurt her tremendously that he'd left without telling her, that he'd left her with Marsh and me.

"Perhaps he left for good," I suggested. I massaged the blood on my hands, but that went nowhere. It was so thick that it was sticky. I wiped my palms on Newt's couch, adding a few stains to his collection.

"No more of that. Just shut the fuck up, Royce. Just quit."

Just quit. She'd reverted to childhood. That was one way to break down. To devolve. She was a forty-year-old little girl. I looked around the room. After a moment, I said, "Marsh was right about one thing."

Anna set her jaw. Renewed tears rolled down her cheeks. She looked wrathful and traumatized. She'd heard the crowbar meet Marsh's skull.

"That's a big TV."

"How could you do that to Wendell?" Anna asked. "Don't you feel anything?"

"He wouldn't stop popping the beer bottle. I couldn't take it. Perhaps I should've warned him. My grandfather used to pop bottles like that. He was supposed to be sophisticated, and yet he'd pop cherry soda bottles with his lips. I hated it."

"I think you're dead inside. That's the problem with you. You couldn't feel anything if you wanted to."

I thought about a Langston Hughes poem and, with contempt, I rolled my eyes. *Life is a barren field, Frozen with snow.* According to the poet, that's what happens when you don't hold fast to dreams. You grow dead inside. What a joke that was. "You're one to talk," I said.

"What did Wendell ever do to you?"

It was a moment to laugh, but I didn't have the energy for it. *What did Marsh ever do to me? What did Anna or Graf ever do to me? Why was I sore? I had no reason. My life was a shit stain, wasn't it? I was a deviant and ex-con, wasn't I? Whatever could make me behave in such a fashion? Perhaps I'm just contrary. Perhaps I'm dead inside. Why don't you just lie down and die, Royce? Anna willed it, Royce. That matters to her. She willed it, and you didn't do it.*

How does one tangle with such a monster? Mentally, Anna had crossed the Rubicon. She was gone. She'd stepped over the edge of her capacity for sanity. I stared at the blank television screen. The windows on either side of the front door reflected in the glass. The thought occurred to me that I'd never owned a television, and, if I went to prison again, I never would. Time would pass me by.

Anna kept on. She practically frothed. "You're psychotic. I really do think you're a maniac, Royce. You've proven it. You'd do that to the whole world if you got a chance, wouldn't you? You'd do it down the line until you couldn't lift the bar anymore."

"We all got our troubles," I said, feeling something akin to wonder at the hypocrisy. The monster believed I was a monster. What'd she think of herself, I wondered. Who'd she think Anna Vogel was? Whatever the complexity, it wasn't hard to boil down the ingredients to a simple response: she believed herself tragic. She had great pity and a lot of excuses for Anna Vogel.

I couldn't stand the anxiety of silence and waiting, so I got to talking too much. "I found that O'Shaughnessy article about me," I said. "The one you kept. It gave me a chance to read it again. You know the thing that made me the angriest about it?"

Anna's eyes were on the front door. The muzzle drifted slightly to my left.

"I never liked that he mentioned my mother and grandfather. He gloated about it. He just did it to be a gossip. That's what he really was, after all. A gossiper. I'm sure you've read it a few times. Do you know what he's talking about when he says there was a scandal in the thirties?"

The gun drifted back into position. Anna shook her head.

"Although he didn't need to mention that, he did. You know my mother is in prison right now? I like to think she's dead, but she's not. You know why she's there?" I let a beat of silence pass. Traffic sounds penetrated the front wall. "They thought she killed my grandfather. Her father. They thought she killed him with poison. She got convicted of killing him." I shook my head. "O'Shaughnessy didn't mention that. To a degree, he exercised tact. You want to know the funny thing, though?"

"What?" Anna asked.

"She didn't do it."

"How do you know?"

I shrugged. "Let's just say my way of knowing is fool proof. She didn't do it." I stared through Anna. "The son of a bitch lost all our money, so she had a reason to do it. I was a kid, more or less, so I let her take the blame. Curious that you're trying to do the same to me, isn't it? Don't think that's lost on me. I get it."

"You're psychotic," Anna said again. "I don't want to hear any more about it."

I watched her. "I'm psychotic, but you're not. You're perfectly reasonable."

"That's the way it is," Anna said.

"I bet you wouldn't have done any of this if you knew what I had inside me." I smiled, despite the pain of it. "I bet I surprised you."

She steadied herself with a breath. I was getting to her, but she hid it.

She lived to be goaded, so I switched tactics and goaded her. After another look around the grimy room, I said, "A romance between you, Graf, and Marsh would've never worked out. One of the two would've grown tired of sharing. It was inevitable. And you're getting older every day. Not like it was when Mrs. was Miss. They'd get tired of you. Graf got tired of you today. Maybe he left you alone so you got in trouble with Marsh and me."

"You won't be glib when Ruben gets back. He'll tell you what we're gonna do to your bitch of a boyfriend."

Although I tried to ignore that line of thinking, dread resurfaced. I certainly hadn't done anything to help Dominic. I'd screwed that up when I attacked Marsh. Perhaps Newt and Graf were picking up Dominic now. There wasn't anything I could do if they were.

"You wait," Anna was saying. "Just wait until Ruben gets back." She held the gun and sobbed. Her thoughts were stuck on spin cycle.

"Remember what I told you that first night?" I asked. "When you had the money laid out like tarot cards?"

"Just wait," she said. "He'll be here with your boyfriend in tow."

"Maybe this is like that old joke between the swami and the reaper. You hadn't really forgotten that skit, had you? You just didn't like it. You didn't like what it meant for us then and there. It was too on point."

She stopped talking, and she looked at me.

"I thought so. Wicked King Death," I said. "That's how he's billed in those skits. But who played the swami and who played Wicked King Death this time? You or me?"

She didn't answer.

It was then that wailing sirens entered the neighborhood. The racket began low and grew louder, grew nearer. Like curious dogs, we stopped and listened. There were more cars than one. It sounded like the hick town's entire fleet. Anna and I made eye contact. The feeling exchanged was one of mutual alarm. I don't think either of us was clear about whom this new development benefited. She was afraid that if she threw away the gun or turned her back I'd attack her, so she held fast.

"Can I get out a cigarette now?" I asked, resigned.

Anna nodded. She lowered the gun but kept her grip firm.

I got a cigarette and lit it. I sank into the couch. "Perhaps they want to check out this television," I said. "Newt probably stole it." Then, feeling nice and cruel, "Where the hell do you think Ruben went? Seems like he left fast. Seems like he knew they'd be coming."

The sirens were blaring now. The din was jarring. It was difficult to think.

"They're here," Anna said, watching the windows. She began to hyperventilate, tracing shapes with the gun muzzle. "They're blocking off the street."

"The whole squad sounds like." I didn't look around to confirm. I got a few more puffs in. To no effect, I tried to relish the time I had left. Unlike Anna, I knew what hell was about to follow. There were a lot of bad things about prison, but the one that got under my skin the most was that you couldn't smoke when you wanted to smoke. You were always waiting. That was your main energy: waiting.

The police knocked against the door once, and then they smashed the goddamn thing inward. It was a flimsy door, and it gave on the first attempt. It had been, I was certain, unlocked. Evening sun poured into the gaping hole.

Anna dropped the Beretta and raised her hands without an order to do so. She was fortunate the gun didn't discharge when it thudded against the carpet. I let the Chesterfield teeter on my lip and raised my hands, too. The first voice I heard was our old friend, Jimmy the Cop. I recognized the nasal twang. He didn't have anything nice to say. He told his partner he'd prophesized this at a diner in a bus depot a couple days prior. He bragged about intuition. The partner grunted cynically. Another cop told me to get on the floor, so I got on the floor.

Anna joined me.

"Maybe Graf played King Death this time," I offered.

Jimmy the Cop stepped on my back for the breach in etiquette. I stopped talking.

"Search the bedroom," one of the cops was saying.

And the cellar, I thought. *Don't forget the cellar.*

CHAPTER TWENTY

While handcuffed in the backseat of a black and white, we listened to a cop named Paul lecture us through the grille. Jimmy drove, and Paul told us what to expect. First, we'd be placed in a holding cell. After a detective questioned us, we'd be taken to the city jail, which was downtown at the courthouse. We could expect a reporter on site, but we were urged to keep our mouths shut. The cops would be nice if we were nice, and only then. I doubted that but said nothing.

The city jail would be our semi-permanent home until an investigation was complete. The gears turned slowly in Huntington, though, so a trial would be months distant, a year distant. A full investigation took time. That remark got Paul and Jimmy sidetracked with a rant about the state police. West Virginia had a bureau of investigation that swarmed murder cases like gadflies. Paul didn't know yet that Cincinnati would intervene, too. The bureaucratic theater to follow would be Byzantine. It was all just noise to me. Paul pointed out the downtown courthouse when we passed it. I didn't feel curious, but I looked anyway. To a degree, Paul was chivalrous because of Anna. Some people are like that. Jimmy certainly wasn't. I'm positive he kicked Anna when she was on the ground at Newt's. She'd vomited and spouted a lot of things about my recent endeavors before getting into the car. Now we sat side by side. Presently, she just cried.

The Huntington police department had a holding cell as large as a drunk tank in the bowels of the main station. The single cell stood at the end of a dank concrete corridor, an underground passage, through which Anna and I were led. Pipes and long fluorescent lights lined the ceiling. Cages protected the lights. No matter the time of year, Paul informed us, the cell was cold and reeked with the tang of black mold.

When we arrived at the caged wall of the cell, I was surprised to find Graf and Newt already inside, waiting, dejected. That warmed my heart. Both men wore handcuffs. This was one matter that Paul had kept silent about. In my mind, Graf would be a state away by now, mashing the gas.

Chagrined and demoralized, Graf looked up from his seat on the long bench. Newt was at his side. Graf said nothing to Anna, and Anna said nothing to him. Their tension, immediately, was a powder keg ready to ignite.

Graf looked at Paul and said, "I get a lawyer. You gotta let me call a lawyer."

"In time," Paul said congenially.

The door opened, and we walked inside. Besides the four of us, the only other occupant was a guard who stood at the back of the cage. He had his arms crossed, and he wore a revolver on his hip. He watched me, and I saw the flecks of a blood knot in his eye. This special precaution was here to keep the four of us from conspiring and getting stories straight. The guard wasn't quite the size of Newt, but he had a hard look. I pegged him for a veteran.

The door locked.

"Remember," Paul said, generally unconcerned, "no talking in here, folks. You'll get a chance to talk one at a time."

"What about a lawyer?" Graf asked.

Paul ignored that. He winked at Anna in a fatherly way, hoping to lift her spirits. Another guard came down the hall and stood outside the cell. He, too, wore a revolver. He also had a ring of keys.

In that moment, taking a seat on a cold metal bench, everything settled with a crushing weight. Anna sat on the opposite side of the cage beside Graf and Newt. I looked across at her, envying that she'd been able to cut loose and vent her emotions. Each of us in the cell, each restrained with abrasive cuffs, felt similar to Anna inside. Given privacy, each of us would've broken down. I looked over at Graf. He was already staring at me, perplexed.

"Where's Wendell?" he whispered.

So much for protecting your own, I thought. *Why don't you call Paul and tell him he missed one?* That told me the direction Graf would take when questioned. He'd throw everyone and everybody under the bus to save his skin. I wasn't surprised. I wondered if his behavior surprised Anna. Probably not. She would do the same. Of the trio, only Newt was noble.

Anna cried ugly again.

I followed Paul's rule and shrugged.

The guard shot a look at Graf. He wagged his head in the negative.

"I get a lawyer," Graf muttered. "This ain't legal." He tried to cross his arms, but that was impossible with the locked wrists. Impatiently, he tapped his shoes against the concrete. Perhaps it was Morse code. I couldn't tell. The man had to talk.

I could suffer a dirty look, so I decided to break the rule of silence, too. "Where'd you go?" I asked Graf.

Graf peeked at the guard and then back at me. He stopped tapping his feet. He lowered his voice even further as if that would appease the man. "They knew my car. They stopped us outside the hotel." He grinned at me like he still held the upper hand. The smile was a knowing one.

The thought, the implication, chilled me. He and Newt had been at The Prichard to pick up Dominic. If that were the case, I was happy to be with them here and now, happy the cops descended on us when they did.

The guard stepped from the back of the cage and stood between us. "One more word," he told Graf, "and your face is gonna look as bad as his." He gestured toward me. "Understand?"

Graf nodded. He sighed and then tried to put an arm around Anna. Again, the cuffs stifled him.

Anna, relieved to hear her husband had not fled, hid her face against his shoulder. Her back heaved.

Graf patted her leg, the only mobility he managed. "We'll get a lawyer," he whispered. He couldn't stop.

Newt, on the other hand, said nothing at all. Unless you watched him, you wouldn't even have known he was breathing. He never lifted his eyes from the concrete floor. Occasionally, he wrung his hands.

We remained like that, alone with our thoughts, for more than an hour. My attempt at comfort constituted a single thought: *At least Dominic is safe.* The idea kept me from feeling sorry for myself. I kept returning to it. It kept me anchored. Graf and Newt had come achingly close to getting their hands on him. I'd never know for certain, but my assumption was this: the two planned to bring Dominic back to Newt's house and work him over in order to persuade me. They would've made me watch as they beat him, and that would've haunted me forever. *Dominic's ending his shift about now,* I thought then. *He has no clue how close he had come to being brutalized.*

I wondered if Dominic worried about me. What had he thought when I didn't come down to the restaurant for breakfast? What had he done? What would he think when my name appeared in the papers? Would he feel he dodged a bullet there, too? That made me sick inside.

Any noise in the corridor reverberated, so all of us took notice when a rush of footsteps sent an echo through the passage. I welcomed anything to break my chain of thought and the tension of waiting. Paul appeared, and, less congenial than he'd been previously, he whispered to the guard. The guard nodded and isolated a key. Paul stepped to the caging, looking at me. He ignored everyone else.

"You," he said, "Pembrook. Get up and come with me. Right now."

I didn't like his tone. Nervously, I stood. The guard opened the door, and I stepped out. As Anna and Graf watched, tension grew.

"What about my lawyer?" Graf asked.

Newt was in his own world and didn't seem to care.

"Alright now. Come along," Paul said.

The guard closed the door and locked it again.

We walked the corridor in silence. When we were on the stairs, Paul asked, "What the hell happened to you? Do you need a doctor?" He sniffed the air, catching hints of Marsh's piss that had dried on my slacks.

"They roughed me up," I said.

Paul watched me, struggling to understand the slurred speech. After not speaking for so long, the cartilage had stiffened again. I repeated myself. It took Paul a moment, but he caught on.

"I was next after the man in the cellar," I added. "You saved me. You taking me to the hospital?"

"If you need it, yes. We will. We need to ask you a few questions first, though. Try your best to talk. We can get you pen and paper if that'll help."

We ascended the stairwell out of the dungeon. The air changed. Paul led me through a busy ward of desks. The cops, a few in plainclothes and a few in uniform, watched us pass, curious. Talking died down as we neared each cluster. I still had my cuffs on, but I looked the part of a victim. Paul walked to an office with the words Chief of Police: Samuel Langley on opaque glass. He knocked, received permission to enter, and then opened the door inward. He put his hand on the small of my back. He pushed me inside.

The office, considering the station of its occupant, wasn't large. It held a cluttered desk, full of documents, coffee cups, and framed pictures, and an abundance of mismatched chairs (as if seating had been pulled from other spaces to accommodate this gathering). A broad window behind the desk was opened slightly, no more than an inch, allowing crisp autumn air inside the smoky room. A man (Chief Langley, I assumed) sat behind the desk chewing the stub of a cigar. He looked more like a politician than a cop. He had salt and pepper hair locked into place, and he was clean shaven. He wore a Windsor knot. The tie was slender and black.

Four others occupied the room: two men I didn't know and a man and woman I did. With apprehension, I looked at Arthur and Genevieve Blum. Genevieve looked out of place and aristocratic, wearing a dark chinchilla wrap that hung at her shoulders and reached her elbows. A necklace with glittering rocks stood out on her neck. She and Arthur were pleased to see me, but my appearance distressed them.

To my surprise, Paul released me from the handcuffs. As

everyone does, I tried to rub the ache from my wrists, which was futile. The cuffs left ringed bruises.

"Mr. Pembrook might need pen and paper to communicate," Paul informed the room. "His mouth is damaged severely."

Genevieve winced.

"That'll be all," Langley said.

"Yes, sir." Paul tucked away the cuffs and closed the door.

I stood there, looking at everyone in turn while everyone looked at me.

Arthur, in a wool suit as dark as his wife's wrap, shook his head in disgust. "What've they done to him?" he asked. The question floated and died without an answer. A look of despair crossed his face.

I decided that he and Genevieve preferred stoicism to self-pity. Stoicism would be the habit of a man like the Count of St. Germain. I lifted my chin and quieted my breath.

The man behind the desk motioned for me to take a seat in the open chair that remained. "Mr. Pembrook, I'm Sam Langley," he began. "Paul will take you to the hospital when we're finished here. Are your ears busted or can you hear well enough? And do you need to write rather than speak?"

"Please," Mrs. Blum said. "If he is suffering, take him now." She looked at me with a depth of concern.

I returned her gaze and attempted a smile. I sat in the wooden chair. "I look worse than I feel," I said. I declined the pad of paper he'd pulled from the desk. "I can manage. The more I talk the clearer it gets."

"Care for a cigarette?" Langley asked.

"Please," I said.

Langley rummaged through his desk and found a pack of Camels. He shook one loose and handed the stick across. A mounted lighter with the head of a tiger stood on the desk. I flipped back the tiger head and lit the cigarette. A stale Camel was better than nothing. I reseated myself, nodding my thanks.

"I knew he would be brave," Mrs. Blum said.

Mr. Blum nodded.

Langley took a final puff on his cigar, and then he placed the nub in an ashtray. The tips of his fingers were yellow from the habit. Smoke curled around him. "I'll introduce you to everyone," he said. He went clockwise around the room. "This is Mr. and Mrs. Arthur Blum. Beside you is Wayne Burton. And this is Scotty Childress."

I nodded at each but said nothing. I didn't know where this was going, and I didn't know if it'd be good or bad for me. That's one reason I didn't desire to put anything in writing, despite their sly efforts. I preferred to remain partially unintelligible. That would give me some space for deniability. Paranoia told me that the Blums were here to bust me as a charlatan on top of everything else, but the looks on their faces didn't suggest such a thing.

"You're obviously in great pain, so I'll keep this brief," Langley said. "Mr. Blum has a—" Langley searched for the word. He looked to Blum for help.

"Spiritualist," Arthur Blum said.

"—Spiritualist group, with the mayor's wife on it, I'll add, and you and the woman in the cell—"

"Anna Vogel," Blum said.

"—Miss Vogel were contracted to do work with this group." Langley stopped, embarrassed. He felt there was something unmanly about speaking about such a thing as Spiritualism. Perhaps he thought the subject sacrilegious. He'd mounted a large crucifix to the wall.

"As mediums," Genevieve provided.

"As mediums," Langley said. "Is that correct, sir?"

I nodded.

"Please say yes or no."

"Yes," I said.

"Okay." Langley looked at Mr. Blum. "Why don't you tell him about Wayne and Scotty?"

Mr. Blum agreed to do that. He cleared his throat. "There are a lot of scammers in your business," he said. "One can never be too cautious when paying for the services of a medium. I do my homework."

Inwardly, I groaned. *Here it comes,* I thought. *Here comes Frank O'Shaughnessy and Mansfield and my mother and all that dirt.*

"These are good men," Langley added. "They used to work for us."

"I hire a private firm to look into prospective mediums. We did that with Millard Hines before you and Miss Vogel, and we did that with Ruben Graf."

Fire them, I thought. *Obviously, they do garbage work.*

"And we did that with a medium by the name of Pearl Nance before any of you arrived in our town. We are very thorough, and we don't tolerate chicanery." He raised his chin at that. I experienced the weight of his stare. "To put it bluntly, Mr. Pembrook, I hired these men to investigate you and Miss Vogel. I trust—"

"—Trusted," Genevieve amended.

"We trusted Mr. Graf's word, but I always go the extra step. Mr. Burton and Mr. Childress run a fine business of private investigation. They have subordinates, of course, but they take on our cases personally. Mr. Burton was to investigate Anna and Mr. Childress was to investigate you."

I looked at Childress. If he'd been on my trail, I didn't know it. I'd never seen him before.

Self-consciously, Childress smiled. He didn't look the part of a private eye. Rather, he had a bookish air, a thin neck, and thick glasses. That image made him look innocuous and made him good at what he did for a living. If you saw him on the street, you would think him an accountant or schoolteacher. Your mind would never go to private detective.

"More to the point," Mr. Blum continued, "they were trailing the two of you the night on which we had our séance. The night," he added, "you contacted our Charlie. The night I tried to get you to stay at our home."

Langley squirmed in his seat, resisting the urge to editorialize. Blum commanded that level of respect. The chief of police was loath to interrupt him.

"Mr. Burton," Blum said, "if you'll continue from here."

Wayne Burton had a harder edge than Childress. He was built like a boxer a few years past his prime, and he had a face to match. I got the sense from his rough features and broken nose that he'd done some minor circuit fighting in his day. He looked like the type of cop who would beat you to death in an alley if no one were looking. You treated him with respect or you got treated, as they used to say. His air was intimidating, the complete antithesis to that of his partner.

"We picked up Graf's Mercury before it hit Fourth, and we followed you to the Wheelwright Saloon," Burton said, matter-of-factly.

That checked out. I was interested.

"Mr. Graf and Miss Vogel went inside, and you began a circuitous walk to Prichard Hotel. Is that correct, sir?"

I nodded. "I'll give you one better," I said. "She's Mrs. Graf. Anna and Ruben are married."

Langley scrambled for a pen and wrote that down.

Burton glanced at Arthur Blum and then back at me.

"Yes, that's correct," I added.

"We got to a pay phone and called Mr. Blum. We told him where you were walking alone. He told us he'd drive out himself, that he wanted to speak to you. Scotty and I kept up with Vogel and Graf. Once they departed the Wheelwright, they met up with this other man, Wendell Marsh, who is deceased now, and proceeded to Ritter Park."

Blum cut in. "You were with me when that occurred, isn't that right, Mr. Pembrook?"

I nodded assent.

Burton said, "Mr. Graf, Mr. Marsh, and Miss Vogel met with a private investigator, independent of our firm, named Mario Girotti. He was from Cincinnati, where all of you have roots. Mr. Marsh, we now believe, arranged this meeting. Mr. Girotti had contact with Mr. Marsh about Miss Vogel a day prior."

Impatiently, Langley asked, "Do you understand what this means, Mr. Pembrook? Is the gravity of it sinking in, sir?" The corner of his mouth lifted in a smile.

I could guess. Suddenly, I felt pretty good about things. I worked on the scuzzy Camel some more. I wiped at blood that had dried like rust flakes at the side of my eye.

"For one, you had nothing to do with Girotti's death," Langley said. "We have witnesses for that, and Mr. Blum says you were with him at that time. However, you want to tell me how you got from there to the face you're wearing now and to a house with Miss Vogel and Mr. Marsh?"

Genevieve said, "He's an innocent man. I can sense that. He is a man of noble pedigree, Mr. Langley."

Mr. Blum agreed.

What can I say? I told Chief Langley everything. He escorted the witnesses out of the office for these revelations. He brought in a stenographer, and I let it flow. I didn't feel like I needed the hospital now. The pain receded. I asked him for a pack of Chesterfields, and he had one of his flunkeys fetch that and a cup of coffee. I told him about Girotti, Millard Hines, and Frank O'Shaughnessy. I even explained in detail how Graf and Newt had murdered Wendell Marsh right in front of me. Of course, I'd swear an oath and testify to that effect. I'd be his star witness.

At one point, despite his disgust about the details I related, Chief Langley told me something that meant more than anything else. It meant more than the truth, and it meant more than whether he believed me.

That was this: Arthur and Genevieve Blum believed me. And they had the power to demand things in Huntington. Blum, I learned, even had a controlling interest in the local paper, the *Herald-Dispatch*. In other words, the narrative was his to shape, and he'd be shaping it.

"You know," Langley said, "this is all a fucking mess, but Arthur Blum is beyond reproach in this town. He has the mayor in his pocket. He has the paper. He has the school. You don't know how blessed you are to have him on your side."

I had an idea.

"Am I being charged?" I asked.

Langley cut the tip from a cigar. He had a small guillotine model that did the work. He flicked the tiger head lighter and then flipped it back down. His reliance on the paraphernalia was almost ritualistic. I liked a man who enjoyed smoking to that degree.

"With what?" he asked. "You heard Mrs. Blum. You're

innocent." A facetious tone lurked behind his words, a subtle hint, but his eyes didn't agree. He played it straight.

"Where'd you get the tiger lighter?" I asked.

Langley smiled. "A gift from Mrs. Blum," he said. "It's from Siam."

CHAPTER TWENTY-ONE

A rthur Blum pulled into the parking lot behind the Greyhound station. The sun was out, glistening against the depot's chrome trim, and it was warm. It was a nice change from the week prior. In fact, it was unseasonably warm to be so near Halloween. It was a favorable omen for traveling. I was still surprised that Blum drove himself around. He had the money to make a chauffeur do the driving for him. Some people, though, don't like that type of treatment. My guess was that Genevieve did, and Arthur didn't. She had a man drive her around, and he drove his burgundy Chrysler Imperial all over town. He liked doing it.

"Genevieve, Audrey, all of us sense a great power in you," Blum was saying. He referred to me as St. Germain now. I didn't protest. Genevieve, for the past few days, had done the same. Audrey Cole Ward, the mayor's wife, had asked me about the merits of nobility. I'd kept all of them entertained with stories, a few of which I repackaged from old adventure movies.

"We would like for you to stay, of course," Blum said. Loosening his grip on the steering wheel, he looked at me sincerely. "Your connection with Charlie is not something easily replaced."

"Charlie will be there," I said, "waiting to talk. He wants nothing more than to talk to you. He misses you."

We sat in silence for a moment, wondering how to say goodbye. I was eternally grateful to Arthur Blum and his wife. They'd saved me. He'd threatened, I found out, to have the mayor can Chief Langley if the department investigated my involvement in the murders any further. A grand jury would proceed for Graf, Anna, and Newt at some point this year. The newspapers were lurid with accounts of all three. When my name surfaced, it was always tactful and careful. I was a victim. I volunteered to testify if the cases went to trial.

I was grateful, and I wanted to thank Blum and give him what he desired, but I didn't want to pretend to be Charlie anymore. The Blums begged me to do a séance on Halloween (a time, Genevieve said, when the veil between living and dead thinned), but I simply couldn't lie to them. I had to move on. So did they.

Blum gave me his address, and he told me to write when I arrived out west. I promised that I would.

"If you ever speak with Charlie," he said, "if Charlie contacts you, you'll tell us?"

I looked out the window at the other cars and nodded. "I'll tell you," I promised.

"You made a great connection with him, St. Germain," he repeated.

Feeling immense guilt, I opened the door. Blum got out of the car with me. A rich man like that, and he went through the trouble of getting my bag out of the trunk, a bag of Italian leather Genevieve gave me as a parting gift. In keeping with her faith, the edge of the bag had a tiny emblem: the seven-leaved saptaparna, which was sacred to Theosophists.

I stood by the taillights and shook Mr. Blum's hand.

"Godspeed," he said.

"Thank you," I said, "for everything."

At that he smiled. He knew he'd pulled strings to get me out of trouble. About that, at least, he wasn't delusional. He smiled, and he turned and got back into the car. Then he was gone.

I walked around to the front of the depot, and there stood Dominic, as promised, waiting for me. He had a canvas bag over his shoulder, and he leaned against a light pole. With the warm day, he was wearing a white t-shirt with the sleeves rolled and jeans and black boots. His dark hair was greased back. His guitar was in a case on the sidewalk.

I wanted to hug him, yet I still had to be careful in a town like Huntington. *They're more accepting out west,* I thought. *Perhaps we'll even live together.*

Dominic watched Arthur Blum ease into traffic and roll to the light. "What a car," he mused. "I bet it set him back $15,000."

"At least. He's got that and more," I said.

"He could've been your cash cow," Dominic said. "He could've been like the old ladies you told me about."

"He's done more than enough for me," I said. "I owe him. He lost his son in the twenties, and he can't get past it."

Dominic watched me. He understood. He didn't push.

"Let's get moving," I said. I grabbed his hand, just for the touch of it, and then let it go.

He picked up the guitar case, and we walked inside.

Jimmy the Cop sat at the counter of the diner, drinking coffee. He had his back to us. Once I spotted him, I tried to sneak by unseen. A large mirror above the bar ensured that wouldn't happen. His eyes were in the mirror, and he turned as we passed. He wasn't here by chance. When Dominic and

I were in the queue to buy tickets, Jimmy the Cop stood. He strolled over.

"Where you headin'?" he asked pointedly.

Although the man didn't deserve to know, I didn't want any trouble from him. "To Louisville," I said. "And then west from there."

"Far away," he observed. "That seems about right." He eyed Dominic and then me again. "Boy, you sure are lucky to have a man like Mr. Blum on your side. You realize that? You should hear what that woman at the jail has to say about you." He looked at Dominic again. "And you. Couple fairies." He shook his head in disbelief, cursing his luck. We were like ants finding shade from the beam of his magnifying glass, finding shelter where he couldn't follow. It made him sick. "I'd have your ass if it wasn't for Blum. Just know we know what you did to Marsh," Jimmy concluded. "And Hines. And the guy in Cincy. And your grandfather. We know it all."

He and I shared a look of mutual disdain. An unpleasant scenario raced through my mind. My heart was fast.

"Next," said the woman behind glass selling tickets.

"That's us," I told Jimmy. "Keep West Virginia safe."

He didn't react to that. Stone faced, he watched as we stepped up to the ticket counter. The lady sold us what we wanted, and she told us which portal to exit for boarding. We walked away from Jimmy the Cop. He watched us, crossing his arms, but he didn't follow.

Dominic laughed, but it was a nervous laugh. He felt the anxiety of trouble on his heels. The guitar case dangled in his grip. "He still thinks you killed Wendell Marsh," he said. He looked at me, uncertain. After all, we still knew one another very little.

"He always will. Anna's trying to save her ass," I said. "She'll go to the grave saying I did that. Saying I did all of them and a hell of a lot more." I looked Dominic in the eye, and I lied to him. Lying is an awful habit once you're comfortable with it. It's hard to stop.

"I've never killed anybody," I said.

They asked for blood, I reasoned. In a way, none of my transgressions counted anyway.

We stood under a canopy, smoking and waiting until the Greyhound was ready for boarding. The sun was nice. I watched faces in the glass, some bored, some sad, and some hopeful. I counted myself among the latter.

Looking at Dominic, a swell of emotion came over me. We discussed Phoenix, he and I, when I regained my composure.

ACKNOWLEDGMENTS

My gratitude and thanks to the following authors for their guidance, support, and friendship:

Michael August

Brian Berry

C.W. Blackwell

Brian Bowyer

R.J. Calder

Wendy Dalrymple

Stephanie Ellis

Stephen J. Golds

Bill Hatfield

Adam Hulse

Derek Hutchins

Sean Jacques

Russell W. Johnson

Zakariah Johnson

Mitchell Lüthi

Paul John Lyon

Regan MacArthur

Remo Macartney

Catherine McCarthy

Ronald McGillvray

Chris McGinley

Tim McGregor

Jennifer Ostopovich

Anthony Perconti

Ron Earl Phillips

M.E. Proctor

Zach Rosenberg

Austrian Spencer

Matt Spencer

Jonathan Tripp

Ilyn Welch

Clyde Wrenn

Ryan Young

Coy Hall lives in West Virginia, where he splits time as an author and professor of history. His books include *Grimoire of the Four Impostors* (2021), *The Hangman Feeds the Jackal: A Gothic Western* (2022), and *The Promise of Plague Wolves* (2023). Find him at www.coyhall.com.

ABOUT SHOTGUN HONEY BOOKS

Thank you for reading *A Séance for Wicked King Death* by Coy Hall.

Shotgun Honey began as a crime genre flash fiction webzine in 2011 created as a venue for new and established writers to experiment in the confines of a mere 700 words. More than a decade later, Shotgun Honey still challenges writers with that storytelling task, but also provides opportunities to expand beyond through our book imprint and has since published anthologies, collections, novellas and novels by new and emerging authors.

We hope you have enjoyed this book. That you will share your experience, review and rate this title positively on your favorite book review sites and with your social media family and friends.

Visit ShotgunHoneyBooks.com

SHOTGUN HONEY
FICTION WITH A KICK